David Skaats Foster

Rebecca the Witch

And Other Tales in Metre

David Skaats Foster

Rebecca the Witch
And Other Tales in Metre

ISBN/EAN: 9783337089672

Printed in Europe, USA, Canada, Australia, Japan

Cover: Foto ©Andreas Hilbeck / pixelio.de

More available books at **www.hansebooks.com**

Rebecca the Witch

AND

OTHER TALES IN METRE

BY

DAVID SKAATS FOSTER

SECOND EDITION OF "THE ROMANCE OF THE UNEXPECTED," REVISED
AND ENLARGED.

NEW YORK AND LONDON
G. P. PUTNAM'S SONS
The Knickerbocker Press
1888

CONTENTS

REBECCA THE WITCH.

REBECCA THE WITCH.

THE ARREST.

I.

ON a quiet hazy morning,
   Glorious morning of September,
In the year which doomed the witches,
   Sixteen hundred ninety-two,
Lay the little town of Salem,
Still and peaceful as the forest
   In its dress of autumn hue ;
Lay the quaint old town of Salem,
Still and peaceful as the harbor
Which the homely hamlet circled
   With an arm of burnished blue.

II.

With its weather-beaten houses,
Framed of solid oaken timbers,
Straight and primitive and gabled,
   Sparsely scattered round the bay;

Each with one square ponderous chimney,
And its doors and windows, staring
　In a Puritanic way ;
Sleepy, grave, and rusty seemed it,
Like a small old English sea town,
Very different from the noisy,
　Thriving city of to-day.

III.

Crag and torrent, hill and marshland,
Salem's stony farms surrounded,
Walls of dense primeval forest
　Girt them like an iron band.
Where the wharves now line the water,
With their buildings and the great ships,—
　With their ships from every land,—
Floated small and curious vessels,
English vessels, queer and ghostlike ;
And with skiff and cabin dotted,
　Stretched a circling beach of sand.

IV.

Save the thin blue smoke that upward
Eddied from the great square chimneys,
At that early hour of morning,
　All was motionless and still.
Homely peace and calm contentment
O'er the hamlet seemed to hover,
　Like the mist above the hill.
Not a hint was there of conflict
With the fearful hordes of Satan,

Of the vague fear which infected
   Staunchest heart and stoutest will.

V.

Yet, the archfiend's deadliest volleys
On the goodly town had thundered,
Many a witch had signed the compact,
   With her name's ensanguined red.
Twenty witches to the gallows,
Fifty more to rack and dungeon,
   Had this evil frenzy led.
Saintly deacons, spotless matrons,
High and low, alike had yielded,
No one knew what man was guilty,
   Still the dark plot thrived and spread.

VI.

And a scene of that strange drama,
Even now, upon this glorious
Autumn morning, was enacted
   Ere the day had well begun,
For a warrant had been issued,
On complaint of divers persons,
   Good and true men, every one,
That the youthful witch, Rebecca,
Might be found and apprehended,
Might be questioned of her witchcraft
   Ere the setting of the sun.

VII.

On the road which led toward Rowley,
Northward, half a league from Salem,

Rose a homely ivied dwelling,
  On the outskirts of the wood,—
Rose a plain, one-storied dwelling,
With a lowly, sagging gable,
  Moss o'er-grown, and rusty hued,
And a door between two windows,
Like the faces drawn by children ;—
And three cloaked and stately strangers,
  On this morn, before it stood.

VIII.

They were men of grave demeanor,
Grave and stern and Puritanic,
Officers of law and justice,
  Acting in King William's name.
From the door-way gazed a young girl
With a look of childish wonder,
  And a white-haired, trembling dame,
Like a very witch of Endor,
Stood and barred the way before them,
With defiant word and gesture,
  And a glance like scorching flame.

IX.

But the doughty marshall Herrick,
Foremost of those grave intruders,
Grew impatient and the good wife,
  With a sombre scowl, surveyed.
From his path he lightly thrust her,
And his heavy staff of office,
  With a threatening gesture swayed.

In his hand he held the warrant,
And he read with sombre accents,
Read the warrant which empowered him
　To arrest the sinful maid.

X.

Of the two, old goody Proctor
Fitter seemed for deeds of witchcraft,
But the court had made no error,
　As this curious tale will show.
Small and slender was Rebecca,
Small and active, sometimes seeming
　Almost like a child, although
Kindly suns of seventeen summers
Had each outline gently rounded,
And to little neck, and forehead
　Given their rich and swarthy glow.

XI.

In the Oriental outline
Of her little nose, the arches
Of her black malicious eyebrows,
　And her proud lip's curve and swell,
There was something strange and elflike,
And her dark eyes shone with trembling
　Light, like an enchanted well.
Gypsy locks, black, wild, and tangled,
Nestled in her neck and bosom ;
On her brown face cast their shadows,
　Touched it with a witchlike spell.

XII.

Thus, we have Rebecca's portrait ;
Roughly drawn and quickly fashioned,
As the silhouettes from paper,
　　Deftly cut in days of old,—
Of the Puritanic maiden,
Type of primness and decorum,
　　Type of nature, fair and cold,
As Rebecca was the image
Of an implike grace and beauty,
Of a dream's unearthly fancies
　　Caught and pressed in human mold.

XIII.

Several years before, in Salem,
All at once, as if by magic,
Had the little black-eyed maiden
　　And the ancient dame appeared.
None knew whence they came or wherefore ;
'T was a dark enigma, shrouded
　　In a shadow strange and weird.
On some small, mysterious stipend,
They had lived apart from Salem ;
Lived a life of deep seclusion,
　　By all good folk shunned and feared.

XIV.

With a brown hand making shadow
For her eyes, Rebecca stood there,
Stood there, with the wild locks blowing
　　Round her small fantastic head.

It was proof, perhaps of witchcraft,
That her glance was proud and mocking
  As she heard the warrant read.
And the final word she greeted
With a peal of merry laughter,
Whereat Herrick's look grew threatening,
  But Rebecca lightly said :

XV.

" I will go with you to Salem,
Valiant conquerors of women !
But for court and law, I care not ;
  Bolts and dungeons, what are they,
To a witch who hath a broomstick ?
Witches have strange arts, and look ye,
  Lest ye feel their power some day !"
At this bold, irreverent answer
Marshal Herrick scowled and trembled,
Cried in wrath : " Good Fenwick seize her !
  Drag the little witch away !"

XVI.

" Hold !" exclaimed the silent stranger,
Who had stood apart, inactive ;
" Hold !" cried he, with voice imperious,
  And a gesture of command.
" Fenwick ! look ye to the beldame !
And most worthy marshal Herrick !
  Bulwark of this sin-cursed land !

Search ye well the house ! for haply,
There be proofs of guilt, and meanwhile
I will lead the witch to Salem,
　　Place her in the gaoler's hand."

XVII.

Tall and graceful was the speaker,
Tall and upright, like a soldier ;
Handsome was his face, yet darkened
　　By a grave and thoughtful frown.
And his great top-boots, and gauntlets,
Leathern belt, and iron sword-hilt,
　　And his cloak of rusty brown,—
All contrasted very strangely
With the velvet trunks and doublet,
With his lace, and stiff-starched ruffles,
　　And the hat with steeple crown.

XVIII.

Captain in the governor's forces,
He had lately brought a message
From the governor, who was absent,
　　Fighting Indians up in Maine,
To Sir William, acting governor,
And chief justice of the witch court,
　　In this year of William's reign ;
And had lodged with him at Salem,
Given him aid, and given him counsel,
So that witches well might tremble
　　At the name of Renald Fane.

XIX.

With his little captive, Renald
Went toward Salem, lost in weighty
Self-communing, while Rebecca,
   At his side, or in advance,
Tripped with step so light and airy,
That its motion seemed like music,—
   Seemed a sort of goblin dance ;
Now and then, at stolen moments,
O'er her shoulder looking backward,
And his thoughtful face regarding
   With a swift and mocking glance.

XX.

And, when Renald's eyes would linger,
Linger sometimes, in abstraction,
On the childish head and shoulders,
   With their quaint, defiant air,—
On the slender, sinuous figure,
Or the little brown ears, peering
   From her wild and lustrous hair,—
Doubtless, then, he asked, in wonder,
If 't were all a mask and semblance,
If the archfiend might have empire
   O'er a form so young and fair,

XXI.

Which, to him, embodied nothing
But the innocence and gladness
Of a sweet New England maiden.
   Then, perhaps, with sudden change,

Would those great dark eyes regard him,
And their ghostly incantation
  All his wisest thoughts derange.
Face and form resumed their witchcraft.
Was it truth? or was it fancy?
In his heart he felt it working,
  Working, with an influence strange.

XXII.

At the meeting of the cross-roads,
Doubtless by this charm o'er mastered,
Renald paused, and thus addressed her:
  " By this sword! it shall not be!
Yonder lies the road to Boston,
Hasten! there, alone, is safety!
  Little maiden thou art free!
Seek the house of Nathan Sargent!
There shalt thou have rest and welcome,
Welcome, harbor, and concealment,
  For the love he bears to me."

XXIII.

" Not so! " answered him Rebecca;
" That would only prove me guilty;
I am no small craven, fearful
  Of a judge's word or frown,
Let me stand the trial fairly!
For a harmless little maiden,
  In this court of great renown,

Nothing has to fear or suffer."
"Let it be so, then!" said Renald.
And they turned, and walked in silence
    Till they came to Salem town.

THE EXAMINATION.

I.

On that autumn day, the twilight
Stealing through the small-paned windows
Of the sombre court-house, dimly
    Lighted up the great square room.
Ne'er before had been such concourse
At the Salem witchcraft trials.
    And the hour's mysterious gloom
Filled each heart with fearful fancies,
Filled the court with ghostly shadows,
Made the rafters and the cross-beams
    Strange fantastic shapes assume.

II.

At the solid oaken table,
With the magistrates of Salem,
Sat a man of sombre feature,
    Look severe, and iron frame,—
Sat the chief judge, old Sir William.
Soldier, magistrate, and statesman,

With a zeal like burning flame
He had fought 'neath Marlborough's banner,
Tricked the Indians, hung the witches,
Spread the Bible at the sword's point,
   All in his good sovereign's name.

III.

In the black cloak, velvet garments,
Ruff, laced band, and silken skull-cap ;
In the face, square-jawed and massive ;
   Grizzled locks, and peakéd beard,
Well the Puritan, the iron,
Stern, relentless persecutor
   Of the Devil's hosts, appeared.
When, with Hale's reports before him,
He had grasped his solid sword-cane,
Scowled with frown of deadly import,—
   Then had witches quaked and feared.

IV.

Though it seemed as if ne never
Had been aught but the resentful,
Dark enthusiast, there were whispers
   Of a time when 't was not so.
'T was a tale of love and sorrow,
Love and coldness and desertion,
   Shrouded in the "long ago,"
When his locks than night were darker,
When he first, in Charles' employment,
Landed in that rock-girt province,
   Land of forest, land of snow.

V.

With Sir William, it was rumored,
There had come a mystic stranger,—
Come a young girl, with the tender
   Beauty of some Latin race.
'T was the story, oft repeated,
Of a maiden's foolish fondness,
   Of her sorrow and disgrace.
For in time his stern ambition
Steeled his heart as with a cuirass,
And he turned in cruel coldness
   From the fair and tearful face.

VI.

Then he sailed again for England,
And the stranger strangely vanished,
No one knew what fate she suffered,
   Or, if known, 't was never told.
This was he, the iron-hearted,
In whose presence stood Rebecca,
   Like a sprite in human mold.
Well his heart might then have softened
Towards the little friendless maiden,
With the haunting recollection
   Of that sweet sad face of old.

VII.

Several hours had swiftly vanished
In that grave examination,
Which the old chief judge had opened,
   Opened thus, with solemn air:

" Thou dost stand accused of witchcraft,
Of strange arts, of league and compact
   Made with Satan, now, declare
Names of all thy dark familiars !
Names of persons thou hast injured !
And, if hellish feast or concourse
   Thou hast joined, say when and where ! "

VIII.

But, these words of fearful import,
Not affirming, not denying,
Lightly had Rebecca answered,
   Answered, with fantastic mien,
Old Sir William's scowl returning
With the pretty scorn and malice
   Of a captive elfin queen.
Like a thing of dream or fancy,
Some sweet picture, or vague poem,
Out of place, she seemed to stand there,
   In that stern and gloomy scene.

IX.

Now and then the grave assemblage
Had been touched and had been softened
By her voice, sweet-toned and pleasant,
   By her childish words and ways,
By her face's sad expression,
As she, through the half-raised window,
   Looked, with far-off tender gaze,

At the clouds and at the sunlight,
At the woods, and hills, and meadows,
Which had been the sole companions
   Of her childhood's lonely days.

X.

But this mask of grace and sweetness,
Mask of beauty, fair and gentle,
While they gazed, would often vanish,—
   Vanish like a flash of light.
Then her eyes grew strange and starlike,
Look and gesture seemed fantastic,
   And her wild locks black as night.
Some mysterious force had changed her,
To an ugly brown-faced wizard,
And they rubbed their eyes and wondered,—
   Wondered if they saw aright.

XI.

Then had witnesses come forward,
With their several depositions :
One had seen her in the forest,
   Bending o'er a crystal well,
Making faces in the water,
Talking to her own reflection,
   As beneath some devilish spell.
Deacon Cloyse had heard her singing,
To their sweet and pious psalm-tunes,
Words outlandish, strange, and sinful,
   Words whose sense no man might tell.

XII.

Heard her singing, with irreverent,
Nasal twang, the sweet and saintly
Hymns of Sternhold and of Hopkins,
    Hymns of quaint and good renown.
Once Rebecca, with her demon
Of a great black cat before her,
    Had been found by Mistress Brown,
Holding meeting in the wood-shed,
With this great black fiend for preacher,
In derision of the godly
    Minister of Salem town.

XIII.

Goodman Pope had once been startled
By a strange and witchlike laughter,
As he passed, one day in summer,
    Though the forest, dim and still ;
Here and there its mocking cadence
From the air above had led him,
    Stumbling, groping on, until
Looking up he saw Rebecca
In a great oak tree, whose climbing
Spoke of witchcraft, and betokened
    More than human strength and skill.

XIV.

Stranger things were then related :
Doves would perch upon her shoulder ;
All the dwellers of the forest
    Answer to her mystic call.

Not alone had brute creation
Owned her sinful fascination,
   For the maidens, one and all,
Had remarked the furtive glances
Of the young men as they passed her.
With her eyes she had bewitched them,
   Had bewitched them, big and small.

XV.

Then had marshal Herrick spoken
Of Rebecca's apprehension,
Of her threats and bold irreverence ;
   How his search had brought to light
Certain damning evidences,
Such as philters, divers broomsticks
   Worn with many an airy flight,
Dolls or puppets pierced with needles,—
These and other tools of witchcraft,
Such as made her guilt apparent,
   Made her guilt seem black as night.

XVI.

Thus, with evening, had Rebecca's
Long examination ended.
" 'T is enough," the old chief justice
   Sternly cried ; " the court decrees,
That the prisoner stand committed
To the prison here in Salem,
   Till such time when it shall please
This high court to give her trial.
Many a witch has decked the gallows,

Many a witch in flames has perished,
　　On less weighty proofs than these."

XVII.

Then Rebecca, for a moment
Seeming, by her look and gesture,
Lost in some wild invocation,
　　Raised her brown, defiant head ;
Dark and proud and strangely fearless,
From those awe-struck men and women,
　　From the solemn court was led.
Near the door stood Captain Renald,
And she turned and looked upon him,
But his face was cold and silent,
　　As the faces of the dead.

XVIII.

Darkness came ; in Salem prison
Sat the little witch Rebecca,—
Sat with head bent down and hidden,
　　In the dark and narrow cell.
Like a figure carved in marble
Seemed she, as the gaoler left her,—
　　As the gaoler fastened well
Door and bar of oak and iron,
That no fiend nor imp might enter,
That no word nor aid might reach her
　　From the subtile powers of hell.

STRANGE DOINGS.

I.

Great excitement and commotion
Reigned in Salem's homely households,
Knots of good men met and lingered,
   Lingered till the hour grew late,
On the green, and at the cross-roads,
In the ordinary's guest-room,
   And with words of solemn weight,
Discoursed of the witch Rebecca.
Spoke of fiends and apparitions,
Spoke of league, and plot, and onslaught,
   Dangerous to church and state.

II.

For, with recent days, had witchcraft
In most curious ways developed,
With a dark and wondrous fancy,
   Most unheard of and unknown.
Now, indeed ! seemed evil rampant,
Now to its appalling zenith,
   Had the archfiend's boldness grown.
Twice of late his apparition
Over truth and law had triumphed ;
Twice the godly ranks, embattled,
   Into fear and rout had thrown.

III.

Goody Good, a witch, arrested
Late upon the night preceding,
Straightway to Sir William's presence,
    Closely watched and pinioned fast,
In the great room of the old house
Built by saintly Roger Williams,
    Strongly built in days long past,
Had been led, there being present,
Renald Fane, stout Colonel Pyncheon,
And three more, and had been questioned
    Of her deeds, from first to last.

IV.

When—as if by magic, quickly
All the lights had been extinguished,
Chairs danced up and down like demons,
    Dreadful cries and groans arose,
On the shoulders of those present
Rained a shower of grievous buffets,
    Shower of superhuman blows.
Then it ceased, fresh lights were gotten,
And behold ! the witch had vanished.
How and where ? no man might answer ;
    Human search could not disclose.

V.

On the night before, still stranger
And more mystic things had happened.
Sergeant Haynes and Master Fenwick,
    Men of metal true and good,

Had arrested old dame Partridge,
And, the wrinkled witch conducting,
   Came, at dark, through Topsfield wood.
They were speaking, as they journeyed,
Speaking words of grace and wisdom,
When, behold ! a dark-faced stranger
   Suddenly before them stood.

VI.

Leaped upon them, like the lightning,
Ere their swords had left the scabbards
Aud with storm of wondrous buffets
   All resistance overcame,
So that through the forest, headlong,
Filled with terror, they were driven,
   And behold ! the wrinkled dame,
So, at least, said worthy Fenwick,
Changed into a beauteous maiden,—
Changed, and vanished with the Devil,
   In a cloud of smoke and flame.

VII.

Strong men trembled, as they listened
To these tales of direful magic,
Yet, the strange narration held them,
   Held them with a mystic power,
Till the night grew late, and fearful
Of the fiend that walks in shadow,
   Seeking whom he may devour,
One by one they hastened homeward,
One by one the lighted windows

Faded out into the darkness,
　And 't was near the eleventh hour.

VIII.

And the gaoler heard a rattling,
Heard a loud, sonorous knocking
At the prison gates, and opening
　Bar and bolt with trembling hand,
Saw the form of old Sir William,
In his great black cloak enveloped,
　Spectre-like before him stand.
" With Rebecca, speech is needful,
Lead me straightway to her presence ! "
Deep and stern his accents sounded,
　And it seemed a strange command.

IX.

But in Salem's narrow dungeons
Many a witch had he exhorted,
Many a witch in secret questioned,
　And the gaoler straight obeyed,—
Led him to Rebecca's chamber,
Left him there, to conjure Satan
　From the sinful little maid.
Time went on, and all was silent,
When, at last, the honest gaoler
Came, to find why old Sir William
　In the dungeon thus delayed.

X.

Lo ! Rebecca's cell was vacant,
All the prison doors were open ;

Once again, had witchcraft triumphed.
   Like a fire the tidings spread.
In the Roger Williams mansion
Old Sir William was discovered
   Snoring in his four-post bed ;
There for hours he had been sleeping,
Caring naught for witch or devil ;
So, at least, his guest and lodger,
   Captain Fane, there present, said.

XI.

Morning came ; all Salem wakened
To this fact of solemn import :
To its wildest consummation
   Had the power of witchcraft grown,
When the Fiend thus masqueraded
In the form and cloth of Justice,
   To defend and save his own.
Fear upon all men descended,
And they walked more circumspectly,
Shunned the darkness and the shadow,
   Went not forth at night, alone.

THE GHOST.

I.

Large and stately was the old house
Where Sir William lodged, at Salem ;

'T was the Roger Williams mansion,
  Built in sixteen thirty-three,—
Built of solid sash and portals,
Brick and glass and oaken timbers,
  Brought by ships across the sea.
'T was a grave, substantial building,
With a single, great, square chimney,
And each end was darkly shadowed
  By a giant linden tree.

II.

Though its shingled sides and gables
Were with moss and mould encumbered,
Well its timbers had resisted
  Half a century's decay,
And each long and low framed story
O'er the one beneath projected
  In the old-time, curious way.
At the meeting of the cross-roads,
Stood it, like some veteran landmark,
Like an old Cromwellian soldier,
  Battle-scarred and weather-gray.

III.

All its rooms seemed cold and gloomy,
With their rows of small-paned windows,
And their low, bare, cross-beamed ceilings,
  Darkly stained with fire and smoke.
In the great reception chamber,
And the dimly lighted hallway,
  Panelled with worm-eaten oak,

Sternly scowled, from dingy portraits,
Divers grave New England worthies,
Endicotts and Smiths and Winthrops,
   Clad in cuirass, gown, or cloak.

IV.

Backward from the larger structure
Ran a gabled wing, connected
With the mansion by a stairway
   And a passage dark, whose door,
Had been ever barred and bolted,
Since the death of some fair lady,
   Who had lived there years before.
For this wing, some said, was haunted ;
In its bare and distant chambers
Lights had sometimes gleamed, and footsteps
   Sounded on the creaking floor.

V.

'T was a sad and rusty mansion,
Filled with rich and sombre memories,
Memories which took shape and substance
   When the storm-winds and the rain
Blustered down the great square chimney,
Made the doors and windows rattle,
   Made each timber creak and strain ;
Or when floods of trembling moonlight
Floated in the great bare chambers,
And the linden's ghostly fingers
   Seemed to knock upon the pane.

VI.

Still more sombre, now, and dreary,
Stood the old house, for Sir William,
Since the night in which Rebecca
    Had been spirited away,—
Stricken with a grievous illness,
In a grim and fearful humor,
    In his great dark chamber lay.
Though he often thus had suffered,
In this sudden visitation,
All men saw the hand of Satan,
    Saw and trembled with dismay.

VII.

Days had vanished, and his sickness,
Which before had always mended
With such length of time, seemed graver ;
    'T was a night of leaden skies,
Night of darkness, flood, and tempest ;
In each corner of the old house,
    Strangest noises seemed to rise :
From the locked and distant gable
Came the sound of sledge-like pounding,
Sound of doors that shut and opened,
    Strangest sobs, and shrieks, and sighs.

VIII.

It was midnight, and the sick man,
Reading in his great oak bedstead,
By a flick'ring lamp, which dimly
    Lighted the vast chamber's gloom,

Seemed to hear along the passage,—
Hear upon the creaking stairway,
    Hear through each resounding room—
Rustling as of silken garments,
Ghostly, slow-approaching footsteps,
As of that fair lady, long since
    Sleeping in the narrow tomb.

IX.

O'er the square and massive fireplace,
Facing toward the open door-way,
Hung a dim, old-fashioned mirror,
    In a frame of tarnished gold,—
Hung a dingy, wondrous mirror,
Of whose mystic power and history
    Dark and curious things were told ;
For, at certain times and seasons,
He, who in it gazed, was startled
By some pallid face, or semblance,
    Long departed, and, behold !

X.

As the glance of old Sir William
Rested on the magic mirror,
O'er its surface came a shadow,
    Changing in a moment's space,
To the dim and ghostly semblance
Of a dark-haired Eastern maiden,
    With a swarthy, oval face,

And a form of graceful outline,
In a quaint, old-fashioned bodice,
Bodice of long-faded satin,
  Stiff with gems and edged with lace.

XI.

And the old man's look grew ghastly,
For the phantom was Giuditta—
Was Giuditta, wronged and martyred
  In the thoughtless days of yore ;
She whose dark, reproachful glances
And imploring words were written
  In his heart, forevermore.
From the dingy mirror, slowly
Faded out the shadowy likeness,
And a vague and rustling figure
  Seemed to pass the chamber door.

XII.

Three times came that wondrous vision,
Came and passed, and then Sir William
Found his voice, and, filled with frenzy,
  Shrieked that long-forgotten name,
So that Captain Fane, awakened
By his wild and fearful outcry,
  Hurrying to his chamber, came.
Strangely taciturn and quiet,
Lost in sombre thought, he found him,
Found his malady increasing
  Like a burning, inward flame.

XIII.

Morning dawned, all day he labored
With a dark and strange chimera :
For the curious doubt had entered
  In his once cold, fearless mind,
Whether all his state and wisdom
Were not like the flower that withereth,
  Were not like the empty wind ;
Whether, really, in his frenzied
Persecution of the witches,
He had acted for the glory
  Of the Saviour of mankind.

THE COMPACT.

I.

In those troublous days, near Salem
Lived a white-haired, saintly preacher,
Samuel Hale, a man of learning,
  And of fearless will and thought.
He alone of all his fellows
Had not joined the witchcraft outcry.
  He alone had set at naught
All those fearful evidences,
And had boldly said that witchcraft
Was a thing of air, a shadow
  From disordered fancies wrought.

II.

For these things he then was resting
'Neath Sir William's stern displeasure,
Though he had been known and honored
    By that great judge many a year.
Strangely, now, to him Sir William
Turned in his dark desolation,
    In this hour of shadowy fear.
And the old man, quickly summoned,
Came without a moment's parley,
Came as though he had been waiting
    For the summons to appear.

III.

With the sick man long he tarried,
Tarried till the grim old justice
Was subdued and calmed and softened
    By his godly words and ways.
Near his bed there lay an order
For a witches execution,—
    Lay an order which for days
Had his hand and seal awaited,
And behold ! as if enchanted,
Suddenly he seized and flung it
    In the hearth fire's smouldering blaze.

IV

Then he told the reverend preacher,
Of that fearful apparition ;
Told the story of Giuditta,
    How in youth and beauty's glow

He had robbed her from her father,
Old Bersezio, by a secret
   Marriage, which no man might show ;
How they fled across the ocean,
How at last he spurned and left her,
Like a fragile rose, to perish
   In that land of rock and snow.

V.

As he ceased, the good-man answered
With an accent strangely fervent :
" In thy power there is atonement,
   Though a mournful one, at best.
Thou must own this secret marriage,
That thy lady's name no longer
   'Neath a cruel stain may rest ;
That her slumber may be peaceful
In that dark and narrow chamber ;
That thy heart may be no longer
   Haunted by its ghostly guest."

VI.

To this act of mournful justice
Eagerly the judge consented.
And to this effect a paper,
   At his own express command,
By the reverend man was written.
And Sir William signed and sealed it,—
   Sealed it with a trembling hand.
And the preacher's gray eyes twinkled
As he grasped the costly writing,

And he spoke, and told a story,
　Like the tales of fairy land.

VII.

Told how this unhappy lady,
Dying in a land of strangers,
Had bequeathed a little daughter
　To his care ; how he alone
Had possessed this weighty secret,
And his smiling charge entrusted
　To an old and faithful crone ;
How, with her, the little maiden,
In a homely cottage hidden,
Ignorant of her name and station,
　To a woman's years had grown.

VIII.

" Tell me that she lives—this maiden ! "
Cried Sir William, "that her mother's
Sufferings in her life may vanish,
　In her joy be rectified ! "
But the good-man, naught responding,
Rose, and with an air mysterious,
　From the shadow, deep and wide,
Of the massive four-post bedstead,
Led a dark-eyed, graceful maiden,
Led the little witch, Rebecca,
　Smiling, to her father's side.

IX.

And the old man gazed in wonder,
For it was as if Giuditta

Had been brought to life—translated
  From that far and shadowy shore.
And a flood of recollections,
Flood of tenderness, swept o'er him—
  Touched his heart's remotest core.
And he cried : " O child of Judith !
Thou art come, like some sweet angel,
Come to be my staff and solace ;
  Thou shalt leave me nevermore ! "

X.

" Not so ! " cried a voice, whose owner
Slowly stepped from out the darkness ;
" For her heart is steeped in witchcraft,
  And a witch she will remain.
With the fiend she hath compacted,
And this fiend, who works in darkness,
  Will his precious right maintain.
From a prison cell he freed her,
And for this, to her deliverer
She is bounden, and hath given
  Her sweet self to Renald Fane."

JANSEN AND PHILIP.

A TALE OF OLD NEW YORK.

'TWAS in New York, a thriving town upon
    Manhattan Isle,
A town of twenty thousand souls, built in the old
    Dutch style,
A town of customs long extinct, whose every sign
    to-day
Has vanished, and whose very walls and streets
    have passed away.
The year was seventeen seventy-six, a time when
    classic lore
And ruffled shirts together went ; when our ances-
    tors wore
Three-cornered hats and long-queued wigs and
    buckles at the knee,
With velvet coats and satin vests, embroidered
    wondrously ;
When debutantes and stately dames astounding
    toilets made,

36

With powdered hair and great court hoops and
    richly flowered brocade.
'T was in September, scattered round in harbor
    and in bay,
With thirty thousand men aboard, the English
    squadron lay.
The battle of Long Island had been fought and
    had been lost,
And Washington from Brooklyn town at dead of
    night had crossed.
His troops were cantoned in the streets ; along the
    Boston road
From dawn to eve a surging stream of exiled wan-
    derers flowed.
Pale faces and the clang of bells, the rolling of the
    drum,
Showed that a crisis was at hand, and that the end
    had come.

They had been friends for many a year, the heroes
    of this tale,
And one was Jansen Schuyler, and the other Philip
    Hale.
The Schuylers were among the first to join that
    fearless band
Of patriots, and to link their fate to their adoptive
    land.
They lived upon the Bowery road ; their stately
    mansion bore
The Schuyler arms in bold relief above the wide
    arched door,

And on its red-brick gabled front the curious fact
    was told,
In iron figures quaintly wrought, that 't was a cen-
    tury old.
The Hales could boast of long descent, of names of
    grave renown,
And Philip's father long had held an office from
    the crown.
Their mansion near the fortress stood, their for-
    tunes were allied
To England's cause, their hearts and hopes were
    on the Tory side.
Between the Hales and Schuylers, thus, the first
    grave difference came,
And Jansen saw his friend no more, but filled with
    warlike flame,
In freedom's conclave nightly sat, and marched
    and drilled by day,
With that small band which Hamilton was forming
    for the fray.

Though like in stature and in age, no eye could
    mark or find
Similitude between the friends in face or heart or
    mind.
The form of Jansen was erect; he had the pride
    and grace
Of a Norse Viking in his step and in his noble
    face,
With its blond beard and fearless eyes of clear,
    straightforward blue.

His life was like his outward form, symmetrical
  and true ;
For passion never swayed his heart, or made his
  mind less clear.
He lived like that proud knight of France, without
  reproach or fear.
Though Philip's face was dark and pale, and in
  itself expressed
No beauty, yet his voice and smile a curious charm
  possessed.
His nature was a medley, formed of contradictions
  strange,
Of noble impulse and resolve, of swift and sudden
  change.
Though often moved and led away by freaks and
  passions strong,
His heart was swift to own its fault, to expiate the
  wrong.
By Jansen's side he thought himself immeasurably
  small ;
And ever leaned upon his friend as on a granite
  wall.

There was a widow, Mistress Clarke, who lived in
  modest ease
In her small villa, hidden quite among the rocks
  and trees,
About a mile beyond the town. They called it
  Falcon's Nest ;
'T was near the site of Union Square, but farther
  to the west.

She had a child whom Philip loved, a maiden free
    as air,
Who filled the place with magic charm, and made
    it bright and fair.
They had been playmates from their youth, and
    't was their childish plan,
That Annie should be Philip's wife, when he be-
    came a man.
She was a gentle, slender girl, brown-haired and
    hazel-eyed,
With form and limbs which could not be ungrace-
    ful, if she tried.
Her mind was pictured in her face by every smile
    and look ;
One read it there as one might read a story from a
    book.
Her voice was soft and musical, but most her
    magic lay
In her quaint smile and in her eyes, which had a
    curious way
Of looking upwards suddenly, and in their depths
    the whole
Of her sweet thought revealing down into her very
    soul.
Her kind heart never knew the pangs those eyes of
    hers had cost,
For he who came within their spell and gazed too
    long was lost.

Philip had often to his friend in glowing words
    portrayed

The charms of face and mind which marked this
    little sylvan maid ;
Had often brought them face to face, these friends
    that he loved best.
A year had passed since Jansen first had come to
    Falcon's Nest.
'T was an unlucky hour, an hour of strange, re-
    lentless fate,
That time, when Philip's friend first passed the
    little rustic gate.
In Jansen's words and Jansen's look a strange en-
    chantment lay,
For Annie's breast was deeply moved, and when he
    passed away
His voice and likeness lingered still, deep in her
    bosom's core ;
She felt she ne'er had lived till then, had never
    loved before.
And Jansen slept not all that night, but mourned
    the curious fate
Which opened up a view of heaven, when it was all
    too late.
But Jansen's heart was staunch and true, and Jan-
    sen's will was strong,
And 'gainst this treachery to his friend he battled
    well and long.
And Philip knew it not ; his eyes were closed to
    every sign ;
He walked, unconscious of the truth, upon a burn-
    ing mine.
He felt aggrieved when Jansen sought to shun that
    dangerous snare.

It seemed to him a strange dislike, and with a constant care
He sought to reconcile his friends, and ever fanned the flame
In Jansen's heart with Annie's praise, and so it often came
That they three sat 'neath Annie's porch in evening's fading light,
And watched the stars and listened to the voices of the night.
And Philip marked not Annie's cheek, nor Annie's heart-beats heard,
When her small hand in Jansen's hand lay like a frightened bird.

'T was now a wild and lawless time; an armed mob scoured the town;
Each day some luckless Royalist, some servant of the crown,
Was seized and tried upon the charge of treason to the State.
It was a dark September night, the hour was growing late,
When some one knocked at Jansen's door, with loud, impatient din,
And Jansen came and drew the bars, and Philip rushed within.
"The mob!" he cried; "they 've burned our home; their leaders thought to find
My father there; and I escaped, and they are just behind."

Breathless and trembling, there he stood, with torn,
    disordered dress,
And Jansen swiftly barred the door, and from an
    oaken press
Took down a dark, old-fashioned cloak, which oft
    in rain and storm
Had sheltered him, and wrapped it well 'round
    Philip's shivering form.
Then led him by the garden path to where his good
    gray steed
Stood ready saddled in the stall, and bidding him
    God-speed,
Flung wide the gate upon the moor, and like a flash
    of light,
Upon the saddle Philip sprang and vanished in the
    night.

The next day saw the town girt round by all the
    British fleet,
Witnessed the landing of Lord Howe and Wash-
    ington's retreat.
So swiftly drew the English lines around by sea
    and land,
That there was scarcely time to fly, and one belated
    band
Was saved alone by Aaron Burr, whose cool, un-
    erring skill
Led them through by-ways, woods, and glens, and
    over vale and hill,
And brought his column safely through beyond the
    British line,

While yet Lord Howe at Murray Hill was sitting
    o'er his wine.
Then came the fight of Harlem Heights, wherein
    five thousand men
Of England's best marched up the hill and then
    ran down again.
Six days the British held New York, and on the
    seventh day
There rose a mighty fire which swept half of the
    town away.
Starting at Whitehall Slip, it crossed upon the
    Hudson side,
And burning northward, left a swath of ruin long
    and wide :
A vast extent of smoking pyres, charred beams, and
    blackened walls ;
No building west of Broadway stood, excepting old
    Saint Paul's.
The maddened soldiers wreaked their hate alike on
    friend and foe,
And thousands, driven from their homes, were hur-
    rying to and fro,
With aimless steps and faces pale, and many a
    wanderer found
No shelter but the Lord's blue sky, no pillow but
    the ground.

Upon the evening of that day a girlish form in
    white
Stood by the gate at Falcon's Nest and gazed into
    the night.

It was a dark and gusty eve, and still a sombre red
Far off above the smoking town across the sky was
    spread.
The young girl's heart was strangely sad, her eyes
    were filled with tears,
And all her soul perplexed and torn with vague and
    gloomy fears.
She thought of all the homeless waifs that cruel fire
    had made ;
She thought of Jansen far away, and bowed her
    head and prayed.
There came a step, a shadow dark upon the path-
    way fell,
And lo ! in his great bandit's cloak, that cloak she
    knew so well,
She saw the form of Jansen stand before her tear-
    dimmed eyes,
And with a little cry of joy, of wonder, and
    surprise,
And that dear name upon her lips, of him that she
    loved best,
She flung her arms about his neck, her head upon
    his breast,
And poured out all her soul in wealth of loving
    words until
Her heart was eased, and then she paused ; but he
    was strangely still,
And starting back, she looked and saw a face un-
    earthly pale—
Saw, wild and ashen as a ghost's, the face of Philip
    Hale !

One moment—all his life crushed down, as by a
    sudden blow—
Stood Philip trembling like a leaf, and swaying to
    and fro.
Fair Annie sought in vain to speak ; she knew not
    what to say ;
And Philip turned without a word and silent, passed
    away.

While yet against the starless sky the smold'ring
    city glowed,
There came the tramp of arméd men upon the
    Broadway road.
Northward they marched, a half a score of grena-
    diers in red,
And in their midst, with pinioned arms, a captive
    spy was led.
The papers found within his vest were signed by
    Aaron Burr.
He had been dogged and pointed out by some offi-
    cious cur,
And taken on the ferry stairs an hour before, and
    now
They led their prize to Beekman house, the quar-
    ters of Lord Howe.
They left the town and skirted then a small fresh-
    water lake ;
Their torches gleamed upon its breast like a long,
    glittering snake.
They gained the Boston road and wound beneath
    a wood-capped hill,

Which then was known as Inclenberg, and now is
  Murray Hill.
And there, a haggard, desperate man stood in the
  shadow cast
By Robert Murray's great farm-house and watched
  them as they passed.
And lo ! he started and his eyes flashed out a
  strange, fierce light,
As scarlet coats and shining arms went on into the
  night ;
For 'neath the torches' fitful gleam, for one short
  moment's space,
He saw the prisoner's blood-stained dress, his pale
  and steadfast face,—
Saw Jansen bound and led along, a poor, inglo-
  rious spy,
And knew that his revenge had come, that his false
  friend must die.

Surrounded by its broad domain of pasturage and
  wood,
Some distance from the Boston road the Beekman
  mansion stood,
And from a rising knoll looked down upon the
  Harlem's blue
From Randall's Island to Hell Gate—a wide and
  varied view.
Of massive stone and brick and oak 't was fashioned
  straight and square.
Within its walls five families might have lived with
  rooms to spare.

Its gabled roof was green with mould, its stories
    long and low ;
Between the columns of its front a recessed portico
Led through a spacious door-way to a hall more
    spacious yet,
Where one might drill a company or dance a
    minuet.
And Beekman house was sadly changed on this
    eventful night :
Its rooms were full of scarlet coats, each window
    blazed with light ;
Deep oaths rang out and sabres clanked in corridor
    and stair ;
For, with his retinue and aids, Lord Howe was
    quartered there.
In the great Beekman dining-room, upon the Beek-
    man plate,
Surrounded by his brilliant chiefs, he dined in
    princely state.
Before him lay the papers found upon the captive
    spy.
The champagne sparkled, and the wit of song and
    jest ran high ;
They laughed at Mister Washington, but they were
    strangely still
About the fight at Harlem and their run down
    Break-neck Hill.
And neither did they mention there, those soldiers
    of renown,
The night they thought to take him as he lay in
    Brooklyn town ;

And how they rubbed their eyes, and saw, when
    morning came again,
That he had slipped away at night with twice five
    thousand men.

The river side of Beekman house was dark and
    still, and there,
Were sentries marching to and fro before a
    mold'ring stair,
Which downward through an oaken door and nar-
    row archway passed,
And led into the Beekman vaults, a stronghold
    doubly fast,
Where, with his head upon his arms, the prisoner
    Jansen lay,
And waited with a steadfast heart for night to pass
    away.
Beside him burned a flickering lamp, whose feeble
    light was thrown
Upon the great decaying beams and walls of cob-
    webbed stone.
He heard the waves beneath the hill, the sentry's
    measured tread,
And now and then an echo faint of laughter over-
    head,
And through it all upon his ear a voice of silver fell,
Before him in his mind rose up that face he loved
    so well.
Hours passed. He heard the sentry's voice without
    the walls, and then
A footstep sounded, and his door swung wide and
    closed again.

And lo ! a mantled stranger stepped within the
    lamplight pale,
And throwing back his cloak, revealed the face of
    Philip Hale ;
He motioned Jansen back, and spoke with hatred
    in his eye,—
Spoke with a quick and trembling voice, nor waited
    for reply :
" Thy papers have not proved thy guilt, friend Jan-
    sen.   Thou art free.
But though 't is mine to bear this word, thy fate is
    naught to me ;
For I have come from Falcon's Nest, and I have
    learned to-night
To know thy friendship as it is, to read thy heart
    aright.
Here ! take thy cloak ! and wrap it well around thy
    face and form !
The night is cold, and there is one would have thee
    safe and warm !
Cursed be the hands that wove it ! cursed the
    hands which spun its thread !
Ere I had taken aught from thee, I would I had
    been dead !
Go ! leave me !   In McGowan's Pass there is a
    sheltered place,
And there, at dawn, must Jansen meet his old friend
    face to face,
And with his good sword prove that he is not a
    living lie—
This world 's too small for him and me, and one of
    us must die ! "

One moment Jansen stood there, all his being
    strangely wrought
By Philip's words, and then he turned and, lost in
    bitter thought,
With his great cloak around him thrown, went from
    his prison door.
The guards drew back and bade him pass, and he
    was free once more.
Yet, as he strode into the gloom, resist it as he might,
There crept a chill upon his soul, a darkness like
    the night.

The hours wore on, and it was strange how Philip
    lingered still
In that sepulchral, mouldy cell, as of his own free will.
Yet there he sat ; within his hands his face half
    hidden lay ;
He marked not how the night sped on ; his thoughts
    were far away.
Save for the tears upon his cheek, the trembling
    through his frame,
He seemed a figure carved in stone ; and when the
    gray dawn came
He rose and, with a radiant face, knelt on that
    pavement bare,
And poured out all his soul to God in one long,
    fervent prayer,—
A prayer for Jansen, for that friend of many a
    joyous day,
For that sweet girl whom he had loved—how well,
    no words could say,—

A prayer that Christ might come to him, and ever
    from that hour
Surround him with his loving arms and with his
    heavenly power,
Might banish envy, pride, and fear, and, like a
    gentle friend,
Support his weak, uncertain steps and lead him to
    the end.

The sun came up above the hills and thinned the
    mist and spread
A glory o'er the autumn woods of glistening gold
    and red.
The frost yet sparkled where it lay upon the blades
    of grass,
And hung like diamonds to the rocks about Mc-
    Gowan's Pass.
And there, upon the narrow road which led to
    Boston town,
Was Jansen, gazing toward the south and pacing
    up and down ;
For there had Philip summoned him to stand at
    break of day.
The time sped on ; upon his heart a growing sad-
    ness lay.
While pondering to himself how best his skilful
    hand might spare,
A rattle, as of musketry, was borne upon the
    air.
And lo ! a courier from New York dashed up with
    breathless pace,

And reined his steed at Jansen's side, and stared at
    Jansen's face.
"They 've shot a spy at Beekman house, the Hes-
    sians of Lord Howe.
His papers doomed him from the first, and rumor
    said 't was thou.
I bear the news to Sterling's camp." This said, he
    spurred his steed,
And through the wood, beyond the pass, sped on
    with wingéd speed.
One moment, like a drunkard, Jansen reeled from
    side to side,
And dazed, as with a flash of light, sank on his
    knees and cried :
"O wretched man ! whose eyes were bound with
    an impervious veil !
Who had a friend and knew him not, a friend like
    Philip Hale !"

Years passed, and after long defeat, that small un-
    daunted band
Had planted freedom's glorious flag throughout
    this whole broad land.
And peace had come again, and in the streets of
    New York town,
Was preparation swift for flight, and hurrying up
    and down,
Among King George's loyal friends, until one
    autumn day
The British fleet weighed anchor, spread its sails,
    and passed away.

And back unto their ruined homes the exiled
    patriots drew,
And took their burdens bravely up and built their
    lives anew.
There was a homely house, which stood within a
    narrow street,
A home which children's steps made glad, which
    tender love made sweet ;
And there, as often as the year brought round the
    sacred time,
Brought round the day of Philip's death, of Philip's
    deed sublime,
All sounds were hushed, the doors were barred, the
    light was faint and dim,
And there was mourning, fast, and prayer in
    memory of him.
His portrait hung above the hearth ; the softened
    firelight shed
A trembling glory on his face, a halo round his head ;
And there at night, when through the room the
    darkening shadows crept,
Sat Jansen and his brown-haired wife and thought
    of him and wept.
They spoke of all the mournful past with voices
    sad and low ;
They knelt upon the floor and prayed that they
    might hourly grow
To be like their lost friend, and that their hearts
    might never fail
In tender sorrow, reverence, and love for Philip
    Hale.

THE NOAH'S ARK.

IN the year—well! that don't matter ; once upon·
    a time there stood,
O'er the hill beyond the village, where the river
    skirts the wood,
A deserted, gabled house, with tumbling porch and
    broken gate,
And a yard o'ergrown with burdocks, empty, bare,
    and desolate.
'T was in autumn, earth lay fair and still, the day
    was almost done,
Golden shone the leaves of elms and maples with
    the setting sun,
As a child of six years, seeming for his round face
    younger still,
Poorly clad came trudging barefoot on the road-
    way, down the hill ;
His unchildlike, thoughtful manner and his dark
    eyes' timid gaze
Shewed he ne'er had played with children, spoke
    of joyless, lonely days,—

Spoke of sorrow, which is saddest when it comes
in childhood's days.

In his face a look of hope sprang up, and vanished
like a spark,
As he neared the old house—found it still so lonely,
strange, and dark ;
Then he knocked, called "Father ! Mother," with
an accent sad and faint,
Which arose, when all was silent, to a wild and
helpless plaint.
Beating on the door with little fists, a never-ceasing
din,
But an echo answered only, from the empty rooms
within.
Then he climbed a twisted apple-tree, which spread
its yellow leaves
O'er the gabled wing, and through a little window,
'neath the eaves,
Peered long time, with childish rapture, in a chamber small and dim,—
For he saw a scene as wondrous as the fairy tales
of Grimm—
Saw a magic scene, like those described by An-
derson and Grimm.

In that narrow little chamber, strangely, plainly
manifest,
In a cobwebbed, dingy corner, darkened by the
chimney breast,

There were elephants and camels, wolves and lions,
    red and blue,
Led by men with gowns and turbans, gravely
    marching two by two.
Just beyond, a Noah's ark was stranded high upon
    the shore,
From whose hold this motley crew had doubtless
    landed on the floor.
Let us leave this strange host marching, 'neath Paul
    Wickford's eager glance,
And explain why he was haunting this deserted,
    cheerless manse
Like a ghost of joys departed, drawn back by some
    magic spell,
Or a ray of sunshine stealing through the grating
    of a cell,—
Like the visits of the angels to Angelico's dark
    cell.

Seventy years before, this house with gables peaked,
    and chimneys queer
Had been built by Gabriel Wickford, and a legend,
    not too clear,
With the mansion strange connected some dire
    curse for shadowy crime
Of the builder, for the Wickfords never prospered
    from that time,
Until Paul's kind father, bent and worn by many
    an adverse wave—
By misfortune, grief, and suffering, found oblivion
    in the grave ;

Then the house for debt was taken, and the mother
    from that day
Paled and sickened, wasted slowly, kissed the child
    and passed away.
They had journeyed to a distant land, so little Paul
    was told,
And the hope of their returning, day by day his
    heart consoled——
With the glorious hope of sometime he was glad-
    dened and consoled.

In a large, strange neighboring household, with a
    grudging will received,
Paul divined not that strange riddle we call death,
    but still believed
In the morning his beloved ones would return,
    when morning came,—
They would surely come " to-morrow," but the days
    were all the same ;
And unnoticed he would wander softly to his
    desolate home,
Wondering if the night had brought them, hoping
    still that they had come.
Tired with knocking, calling, listening, he would
    climb at last and gaze
Through the little chamber window at those joys
    of brighter days—
At the Noah's ark which somehow had escaped the
    sheriff's hand.
There they often found and led him from the realms
    of fairy-land—

Tore him from the secret treasure, childish faith of
    wonderland.

Leafless were the trees, and snowflakes on the chilly
    winds were tossed,
And the child more sad and lonely, for his faith
    was partly lost,
Since they shewed him in the churchyard where
    the graves lay side by side,
Came once more and knocked and waited, and at
    last sat down and cried—
In the doorway—softly, mutely, wept away his child-
    ish woe.
Darkness came ; the little figure lay there still, all
    white with snow ;
But his lonely heart was happy, in that slumber
    calm and deep,
For he heard dear, loving voices calling to him in
    his sleep—
Heard quick footsteps, saw the windows lighting up
    the wintry night,
Saw the door ajar, and father, mother, radiant with
    delight,—
Sprang into their tender outstretched arms with
    quiverings of delight.

Twenty years had come and vanished, and the old
    house, which had stood
Winter, summer, storm and sunshine, in the drear-
    iest solitude,

Was transformed, as by a fairy, to a castle quaint
    and fair ;
Ivy climbed o'er porch and gables, flowers were
    blooming everywhere ;
And the fairy who had changed it was a maid of
    mortal mould,
Only daughter of the tenant, who had leased this
    castle old ;
And this tenant was the preacher in the village
    church, whose spire
O'er the hill, among the elm trees, at the sunset,
    gleamed like fire.
Several years in calm seclusion they had lived
    there all alone,
And than Madeline, no thriftier housewife in the
    land was known—
Never prettier, gentler maiden, than sweet Madeline
    was known.

And her beauty grew, the longer one beheld her,
    for she stole
Like an animated picture, or like music on the
    soul :
Cheeks, smile dimpled, all her gestures poems, with
    a magic change,
Either loving, roguish, sprightly ; or perhaps in
    contrast strange,
One beheld her sweet, grave profile, bending o'er
    some well-worn book,
With her hair a saint-like aureole, a Madonna's
    thoughtful look

In her eyes, expressive, downcast, or those eyes in
    the romance
Of a girlish revery gazing, with a far-off tender
    glance.
She had passed a happy girlhood in the old house,
    and it seemed,
With its pleasant nooks and corners, where she
    lived and toiled and dreamed,
All her own, like those quaint fancies, those bright
    castles she had dreamed.

And a message from the owner made a flood of
    bright tears come,
Filled her tender heart with sorrow,—they must leave
    the dear old home,
For a stranger wished to buy it, and that very day,
    by chance,
In her father's absence came he, to inspect the queer
    old manse.
He was young and grave and handsome, tall and
    brave as knight of old,
Who awoke the sleeping princess, when the hundred
    years were told.
In his smile was something mystic, what it was she
    could not say,
As through all the curious mansion's dear old rooms,
    she led the way,
From the cellar to the attic, pausing then, before
    the door
Of a locked mysterious chamber, which she ne'er
    had shown before,—

Like that chamber in her heart, in which no eye
    had seen before.

Here she hesitated ; then her fair cheek took a
    deeper shade,
As the door she softly opened and a tiny room dis-
    played,
Desolate and bare and lonely ; and the stranger's
    swift glance fell
On the little wooden figures and the ark, for strange
    to tell,
There they stood, arranged exactly for a march
    across the floor,
As when little Paul last saw them, more than twenty
    years before.
Then with downcast eyes and trembling voice and
    look of maiden shame,
Told she, how a little boy named Paul had lived
    there ere they came,
And how, left alone and wandering through the
    mansion old at will,
She had found these toys arranged, as if their owner
    lived there still,—
How she wept to see them standing there, so sad
    and poor and still.

And these treasures, which so long ago had
    thrilled a little heart,
In her eyes appeared so sacred, that she kept the
    room apart,

And till now no one had ever come into its deso-
    late gloom,
Which the ghost of vanished childhood filled as
    with some sweet perfume.
Here she oft had loved to picture this child's life
    so like her own,
Till, between her and the little Paul, a friendship
    sweet had grown.
He would think it strange, and laugh to hear this
    fancy queer and wild,
But no words could ever tell him how she loved
    that little child.
Then she felt her hand grasped tightly, felt a tear
    upon it fall ;
In her heart strange fancies mingled, of the stranger
    and of Paul ;
Said the stranger : " I would have you love him
    always,—I am Paul."

MARIQUITA.

LIKE a sleepy Spanish village,
    Lay the town of St. Augustine,
With its palms and white-walled gardens,
And its curious Spanish fortress,
Built with tower and moat and dungeon,
In the days of King Fernando.

Half a mile beyond the city,
On the San Sebastian River,
Stood the great old-fashioned mansion,
Stretched away the rich plantation,
Of the fair and youthful widow,
Leonora, Cid y Guerra.

She was strange and wild and tender,
Strange and wilful and fantastic ;
Many a suitor wooed her vainly,
Till, at last, came Dick Van Keuren—
Came, preceded by a letter,
From her kinsmen in Savannah,

On the night of his arrival,
Seeking Leonora's dwelling,
He was led, by sounds of music
And of laughter, to the fortress—
Led to join the merry dancers
At the ball in fort San Marco.

In the fortress' broad enclosure,
Colored lanterns, Strauss' music,
Mingling with the voice of ocean,
Towers and battlements dark-outlined
'Gainst the starry roof of heaven,
Made it all seem like enchantment—

Made it arabesque and dream-like ;
But with him 't was all unnoticed,
For his heart was deeply wounded
By the eyes of Mariquita,
Mariquita, sad and wistful,
Standing statuesque and silent,

Like the ghost of some fair Spaniard
Of the days, of seventeen hundred ;
Standing, where he first beheld her,
In the archway's gloomy shadow,
Whence, with merry jests and phrases,
He had sought, in vain, to tempt her.

When at last to words more tender
He had come, the night was waning,

And the lights went out, the music
Ceased to dull the ocean's murmur,
And the ghostly Mariquita
Fled away into the darkness—

Fled away and like a phantom,
Many a day his search eluded.
Then he thought of Leonora;
Stood at last within her garden.
"Sir, my mistress still is absent,
She will come again to-morrow,"

Spoke the rosy little handmaid
From the doorway, where her slender,
Rounded figure seemed a picture
In a frame; her eyes were downcast,
And she blushed that thus he found her,
For, behold! 't was Mariquita.

Balmy winds of evening rustled
Through the orange-scented garden;
O'er the plashing of the fountain,
And the swaying of the hammock,
Low and tender voices sounded,
Paused and ceased and then continued:

"Do not ask me! oh! I fear them,
Uncle Juan, Uncle Pedro,
And the haughty, cruel cousin,
Leonora, Cid y Guerra.

She was born to joy and riches,
I—to sorrow and to bondage."

Night came on, a white-robed figure
Through the garden swiftly glided
To the thicket, by the river,
Where the steed and rider waited ;—
"Up ! away ! and now forever
You are mine, sweet Mariquita."

" Do you hear that hollow murmur,
Like the distant tramp of horses ?
We are followed.   Oh ! I fear them,
Uncle Pedro, Uncle Juan.
Faster still ! the preacher lives there
Where that light shines out before us."

Strangely, gleamed the flickering torchlight
On the hurried midnight wedding
And 't was then, that Dick Van Keuren
Found that Mariquita's story
Of the proud and cruel cousin,
Uncle Juan, Uncle Pedro,

With the hurried flight at midnight,
And the horsemen following after,
Was a strange conceit and fancy,
A romantic whim, of Donna
Leonora, Cid y Guerra,—
Found that she was Mariquita.

THE OLD SPINNING-WHEEL.

THROUGH the intricate maze of its pulleys and
    wheels,
And its oaken frame, a vision steals
Of the long gone years, of the hands that are still,
And the elm-shaded house at the foot of the hill,
Where the child, round-cheeked and wond'ring-
    eyed,
Watched the old wheel buzz at the ingleside,
With a sound like a far-off muffled drum,
In its " *clickety, whir-r, whir-r, hum.*"

Years come and go ; on the porch it stands,
And the pirns fly round 'neath a fair girl's hands ;
She watches the sunset's fading rays,
With a far-off, girlish, fanciful gaze,
Till the rose steals into her dimpled cheek,
And the garrulous spinning-wheel seems to speak
Her foolish thoughts to Christendom
With its " *clickety, whir-r, whir-r, hum.*"

Still time speeds on ; 't is a winter's night,
The hearth fire is circled with faces bright,
There is laughter and jest, and the storm, in vain,
Beats on the door and the frosted pane,
And the wheel spins round with a measured rhyme,
Like a quaint refrain of the old, glad time,
Like a presage of sorrowful days to come ;
In its " *clickety, whir-r, whir-r, hum.*"

Its voice oft brought the sick child rest,
And lightened many a weary breast ;
Beneath its song the whispered word
And kiss of lovers passed unheard.
If it could speak, that strange old wheel
What wonderful secrets it would reveal !
What romance is hid in the weary sum
Of its " *clickety, whir-r, whir-r, hum* " *!*

It had its influence and its share
In every joy and every care ;
Fast, fast it flew, yet with swifter rate,
Spun round and round, the wheel of fate.
They fashioned out of its woven thread
The dress of the bride and the sheet for the dead,
And the wheel went round, though the heart grew
    numb,
With a " *clickety, whir-r, whir-r, hum.*"

All are vanished and all are still,
And the spinning-wheel by the clattering mill

Has been left behind with the primitive days
Of homelier toil and more honest ways ;
Yet, oft through the night, and out of the gloom
And the gathered dust of the lumber-room,
Its song, like a ghost's voice, seems to come,
With a " *clickety, whir-r, whir-r, hum.*"

SUMMER THOUGHTS.

UPON a mossy knoll in the forest, I
    Lay looking upward at the eternal blue
Of the infinite and quiet heavens, through
The oak-leaf and the hemlock's canopy.
And now and then a cloud went drifting by,
    Listless and slow and changing to the view.
    How like my fleeting summer thoughts to you,
Calm, peaceful clouds !   And now the evening sky
A deeper, darker, lovelier azure hath,
    The birds have ceased their singing, and the
        breeze
Is filled with hum of insects ; darkness saith—
    With the first few stars twinkling through the
        trees—
That night has come.   A little while, and death,
    Like night, will end life's summer reveries.

GALATEA.

I STOLE forth from the merry festival,
  With which the panes of Wentworth glimmered
    bright,
  And wandered in the still midsummer night,
Through an old garden with an ivied wall
And winding paths and statues mythical.
  A pensive marble goddess robed in white,
  Like some fair vision of the shadowy light,
Inspired me with the thought fantastical,
To kneel before her and apostrophize
  Her loveliness in quaint, impassioned tone.
But, starting from her mystic reveries,
  Ere I had ceased, the imagined nymph of stone—
A swift dissolving dream of laughing eyes,
  A magic dream of golden hair—had flown.

THE READING OF THE TALE.

WE read together on a winter's night
    The oldest, quaintest, saddest of romances.
  She leaned upon my chair ; by slow advances
My arm around her stole ; the panes were white
With silvery frost ; the hearth fire flickered bright ;
  My heart was filled with ardent, wistful fancies,
  And in her face I read by stolen glances
A gentle sorrow mingled with delight.
Her moistened eyes looked up ; the tale had
    wrought
  Upon us both love's tenderest, sweetest spell.
She must have guessed my fond and longing thought,
  For her dear head upon my shoulder fell ;
And in that blissful silence there was naught
  Beside the exquisite truth we knew so well.

THE PORTRAIT.

"BEAUTY of yonder portrait! 't is from thee
    That thy descendant hath the loveliness
      Of her arch smile, and blue eyes' thoughtful-
        ness.
Telling thy tale, she bade me laughingly
Beware thy ghost."   Thus lost in revery
    I heard the rustle of a silken dress,
    And saw what seemed the ghostly ancestress
Enter my lonely chamber stealthily.
Close by she passed, a little hand I caught,—
    'T was snatched away,—she vanished into air,
Leaving a ring so small its size with naught
    But Cinderella's slipper might compare,
Which, strange to say, when like the Prince I sought
    An unknown bride, one hand alone could wear.

THE CRICKET.

OH ! little cricket, that the evening long
    Dost tell thy story to the silent hours,
  While the dew falls upon the thirsty flowers !
What is the burden of thy ceaseless song ?
A tale of love ? or secrets that belong
  To the dim solitudes of ruined towers,
  Whose crumbling walls the ivy leaf embowers ?
Or drolleries of Titania's shadowy throng ?
Thou art a friend, so ancient legends tell,
  That with the power of mystic sorcery
Guardest the hearth where thou dost love to dwell,
  And with thy quaint and pleasant company
The night's deep loneliness thou dost dispel,
  Thou merry chief of insect minstrelsy !

THE ROSE.

I PLUCKED a rose that bloomed in solitude,
  Filling with fragrance a secluded bower,
  And saw its petals, falling in a shower,
Rise up a maiden, her sweet attitude
And slender form and dimpled cheek imbued
  With all the grace and beauty of the flower.
  "Art thou," I asked, "the sport of magic power,
Or some dark-eyed enchantress of the wood?"
"A hundred years," she answered, "'t was my
    doom,
  Because I laughed at love and lovers' woes,
A full-blown rose in loneliness to bloom;
  Who plucked the flower and broke my long
    repose,
Him I should wed. Alas! I must resume,
  If he refuse, my sleep within the rose."

THE VOICES OF THE WOOD.

HE, who in some cathedral, gray and old,
    Has cherished solemn reveries, knows the
      thrill
Which moves my heart, in forest dim and still,
Until I long, within the shady wold,
To dwell, and naught beyond its walls behold,
    Save what some shifting, leafy opening will
    Disclose of waving grain, blue sky, and hill,
Village half hid, or church spire, tipped with gold.
With the half gloom of those vast aisles imbued,
    Let me forget myself, in revery,
Till sunlight by their shadow is subdued,
    The breezes hushed by their solemnity,
And like mysterious voices of the wood,
    Religion, love, or sorrow speaks to me.

AN AUTUMN FANCY.

SUMMER has fled, and though the earth displays
  Her woods and fields, her vales and mountains,
    dressed
  In quiet, perfect beauty, on the breast
Of nature a mysterious sadness weighs,
And there doth steal upon me, while I gaze
  Upon the white clouds, floating to the west,
  And sinking 'neath the blue hill's wooded crest,
Once more, the sweet belief of childish days,
That, could I pass beyond yon distant hill,
  There would I find the summer once again,
With skies eternal, cloudless, deep and still,
  And that this bright and beautiful domain
Would give me back sweet friends, and would fulfil
  All hopes and wishes cherished long in vain.

A WINTER FANCY.

THE night wind moans, the frost is on the pane,
 And by the flickering hearth fire manifest
There ever sits a sad and silent guest,
For I the ghost of childhood entertain
And live the days of childhood o'er again,
 Until the thoughts of those, whose kindness
  blessed
 My little world, long vanished, fill my breast
With a great longing, passionate, childish, vain,—
A longing for the arms that round me twined
 And filled my little heart with fond delight,
The looks which every cloud with silver lined;
 The cheering words which made the days so
  bright.
Friends of my childhood! gentle, true, and kind,
 Where are ye all, upon this winter's night?

AT BREAK OF DAY.

THE stars fade slowly, twinkle, pale and die,
  Before the halo rising in the east,
A rosy glamour steals athwart the sky,
  And grows to flames of gules and amethyst,
  The hills are silver-rimmed, the curtain of mist
As at some swift command, rolls back from field,
  Valley and lake and wood, and floats away,
And the whole glorious pageant is revealed
        At break of day.

There is a solemn murmur of the breeze,
  There is a ripple on the lonely shore,
A solitary chirp, among the trees,
  Is taken up and echoed o'er and o'er
  And dies away, and all is still once more.
Then comes the signal, and all living things
  Raise up an anthem, glorious, blithe and gay,
And the whole earth with one grand chorus rings
        At break of day.

There is a night of sorrow and unrest,
   A darkness of the soul—a night when all
The world of thought is haunted and oppressed
   And hemmed about, as with a dungeon wall,
   When heaviness and fear upon us fall.
Take courage, then! the longest, darkest hour
   Comes just before the first faint tinge of gray,
And sadness has no place, and fear no power,
      At break of day.

And when that last, that silent, starless night,
   Comes over us, when the dark, sorrowful stream
Sweeps at our feet, in dread, relentless might,
   And every deed and word and thought shall
     seem
   To pass before us, in a troubled dream,—
What joy! to watch the faintly outlined shore
   Rise, grand and glistening, 'neath morn's silvery
     ray
To know that night departs for evermore
      At break of day.

THE HAUNTED HOUSE.

RUSTY, worn, and stained by wind and weather,
    Still the same, through all the years' swift
    change,
Long has stood a homely, gabled dwelling,
    Silent, dark, and strange ;
Seeming lost, o'ershadowed and forgotten,
    In the busy street.
But 't is filled with bright and quaint illusions,
Hallowed by sweet faces long since vanished,
Haunted by the tread of unseen feet.

He who lives there, careworn, gray, and lonely,
    He who loves its melancholy gloom,
Sometimes hears the noise of children romping
    In some distant room—
Merry ghosts of hide-and-seek, whose voices
    Lead him on, until
Something tells him they are but the phantoms
Of his childish hopes and creeds ;—then swiftly
They have fled, and all again is still.

From his mid-day reveries he is startled
  By a fair ghost, from an old romance,
With a merry laugh, a slender figure,
      And a roguish glance.
Was it all a dream? but look! the curtain
      Trembles still, ah! well!
'T is not true, for her sweet voice is silent,
She has long been sleeping in that palace
Where no knight can come to break the spell.

There 's a whispering in the embrasured casement,
  When the dusk comes and the night winds sigh ;
'Gainst the panes a little group seems shadowed,
      Ghosts of long gone by,
When the mother called her children round her,
      Held them close, and told
Stories of the stars and of the fairies,—
Magic stories, which, in childhood's kingdom,
Change the earth—the very hours—to gold.

But at midnight, when the street is silent,
  And the firelight floats upon the walls,
Quickly all is changed, a bright enchantment
      On the old house falls ;
Bringing back the beauty and affection
      Of the golden years,
Bringing back the perfumes and the music,
Bringing back the faces and the voices,
Bringing back the smiles without the tears.

SANTA TRINIDAD.

REMEMBEREST thou the mission, with its
      memories
    Of times long passed away?
And how, admitted by a solemn verger,—
    A verger bent and gray,—
Thou! fairest Helen! lingered in the garden,
    While I, of graver mood,
Explored at will the queer old Spanish ruin's
    Historic solitude?

There Sister Trinidad, in seventeen hundred,
    A young and pious soul,
Becoming Santa Trinidad, 't was written,
    Put off her hood and stole.
There still were shown the holy vestments ; gazing
    Upon those relics quaint,
My heart grew tender, with the recollection
    Of the sweet nun and saint.

The sunlight, stealing thro' the painted windows,
    Streamed on the chapel wall :

I saw, in a kaleidoscopic medley,
    Its colors rise and fall ;
I saw, upon the altar piece, its radiance
    Restoring once again,
The old-time glory and the beauty faded
    Long since from mortal ken.

At length, from cell and corridor emerging,
    I climbed the belfry tower,
And thinking of those strange traditions, lingered
    Until the twilight hour :
Returning then, along the shadowy cloisters,
    Mysterious and dim,
I seemed to hear, in mellow cadence, floating,
    The solemn vesper hymn.

I gained the chapel ; thro' the ivied windows
    Yet stole a feeble gleam,
And lo ! as still as marble, as romantic
    As youthful painter's dream,
Bringing me back to centuries departed,
    To thoughts of things divine,
Behold ! a slender, black-robed nun was kneeling
    Before the dingy shrine.

The phantom rose, a graceful, girlish figure,
    With cowl of monstrous size ;
I caught a transient glimpse of pretty features,
    Of two dark Spanish eyes ;
She moved, she spoke, words of soft, foreign accent
    Came from that sombre hood,

The door beyond her opened, in the doorway
　　The ancient verger stood.

One glance he gave—one swift, wild look of terror,
　　As if he saw the dead,
And crying, " Santa Trinidad," behind him
　　He slammed the door and fled.
O laugh more musical than e'er was uttered
　　By recluse grave and sad,
O faithless Helen ! to have donned the vestments
　　Of Santa Trinidad.

THEN AND NOW.

MANY, many years have fled
 Since this land I journeyed through ;
Round the careless youngster's head
 Straggling locks of brown hair blew ;
Laughing, like the fields of May,
 Stretched my future ; though around
Many a dream-like picture lay,
 Tenderer charms in thee I found.

Little maid of fifteen springs !
 As we strolled 'tween wood and stream,
Hours were golden, hope had wings,
 All was like an airy dream.
Now through this same land I wend,
 'T is a memory-haunted way,
Life is hastening toward its end,
 Heart is sere and head is gray.

From thy cottage gleams the light ;
 Childish voices, glad and sweet,

Outward float into the night ;
   At the door thy child I meet.
Little maid of fifteen years,
   So like thine her sweet traits seem,
That my eyes are dim with tears—
   All again is like a dream.

No ; 't is not a dream, for all
   We have lived, worked out, and thought
Is not fabric that will fall—
   Shadow that will come to naught.
What our tender thoughts once hold
   Hallowed, beautiful, sublime,
Ne'er will vanish, ne'er grow old,
   But live on to endless time.

THE OLD, OLD HOME.

MY heart is saddened, for all
 Seems so queer and common and small,
 As I stand by the old house once more.
The gables are not so tall,
 Nor the lawn as wide as of yore,
And the faces that I recall
 Look not from window or door.

A railroad crosses the leas,
And they 've laid out a street where the breeze
 Rustled once in the waving corn.
Oh ! 't is hard to believe that these
 Were the haunts of life's sunshiny morn,
And that those great, spreading elm-trees
 Were planted when I was born.

The old place has changed, and they
Who endeared it have passed away ;
 But still in my heart I behold,
As if it were yesterday,
 The apple-trees, gnarled and old,
One mass of white blossoms in May,
 And in autumn, weighted with gold ;

The meadows, the fields of grain,
The barn, with its copper vane,
   And dovecote under the eaves ;
Where we heard the pattering rain,
   As we lay in the yellow sheaves ;—
And a changing, fanciful chain
   My sorrowful memory weaves :

Of the lilac tree, and the bloom
Of the roses, whose faint perfume,
   Floating in on the breeze, would fill
My dear little narrow room ;
   Of the twilight so soft and still,
The evening's deepening gloom,
   And the moon rising o'er the hill.

My little playmate is dead ;
He died when I met in his stead
   The careworn man : and the mirth,
The joy of the morning has fled ;
   And the dear old home of my birth,
Of my innocent childhood's tread,
   Has passed away from the earth.

But oft in the world of dreams
It exists again, and it seems
   More hallowed, rosy, and quaint.
From my far-away childhood streams
   An aroma, sweet and faint,
And around it a radiance beams,
   And a charm that words cannot paint.

MY FRIEND.

TO him who counts the clock's slow ticking,
　　While the night's long hours wear away,
There comes a truer, nobler impulse,
　　Than aught that moves the heart by day,
And tender fancies, that, like fairies,
　　Fade with the dawn's first streaks of gray.

And so, to-night, while vainly seeking
　　Oblivion from my cares and fears,
There comes a flood of recollections ;
　　A face, which fills my eyes with tears ;
A longing, passionate and childish,
　　For my true friend of boyish years.

And wond'ring what have been his fortunes
　　In the long years since we have met,
I fear his life has not been brighter
　　For my poor influence, and regret
That in the account of our affection
　　I 'm still so greatly in his debt.

I long for our dear confidences
   In those familiar, sacred haunts,
To have once more our golden visions,
   With all their treasures of romance—
The girls we loved, the stately castles
   Which filled the future's bright expanse.

And though those castles all have crumbled,
   Those hopes and dreams have all proved vain
The thought of our sweet friendship softens
   The disappointment and the pain ;
And so, when thinking of my boyhood,
   The tears are dried, the smiles remain.

And though the flood that rolls between us
   Has widened with each year's swift flight,
These kindly fancies, like a rainbow,
   Once more its distant shores unite ;
And o'er this airy bridge returning,
   I 've been with my old friend to-night.

AT ALDEN'S.

WE were sitting by the chimney,
  In the hearth fire's flickering light,
On the cliff, in Alden's cottage,
  Where I rested for the night;
And I told the scenes and customs
  Of the lands beyond the sea;
While old Alden's little daughter
  Sat and listened at my knee.

In her blue-eyed radiant beauty
  There was something shy and wild,
And the maiden's romance mingled
  With the wonder of the child.
Hours had passed, the old sea captain
  In his arm-chair dozed and dreamed,
Sadly moaned the neighboring ocean,
  'Gainst the panes the firelight gleamed.

Then she spoke of knights and tourneys,
  And her cheeks were all aglow,

For all day that little maiden
   Had been reading " Ivanhoe " ;
Spoke of ghosts and of magicians,
   While her voice to whispers grew,
Toward the panes cast startled glances,
   Wondered if such things were true.

And I improvised a story
   Fit for such a place and hour—
How, for long years by the ocean,
   In a cruel fairy's power,
Lived a little maid enchanted,
   Till her faithful knight, one day
While her guardian fierce was sleeping,
   Stole that little maid away.

As I spoke, her blue eyes twinkled
   With a merry, mystic light ;
As I spoke, she rose and lingered
   In the door to say " Good-night."
But her lamp threw such a radiance
   'Round the roguish, pretty head,
That I swiftly stooped and kissed her,
   And she blushed and laughed and fled.

When I came once more to Alden's
   I beheld a mournful change,
For the little maid had vanished
   And the house seemed sad and strange.
Alden's pale, gaunt look foreshadowed
   What his quivering lips would say,

And I grasped his hand in silence
And in silence turned away.

All the proud and cherished structures
By a life-long patience wrought,
All the triumphs which have followed
Days of toil and nights of thought,
Crumble, sink away, and vanish,
Like the ocean's shifting sand.
When that sweet face comes before me,
That lost dream of fairy-land.

ON THE DEATH OF A CHILD FOUR YEARS OLD.

I KNEW a child whose little feet had wandered
    Through naught but flowers, and who—
Still thinking that could he but climb the moun-
        tains,
    He 'd touch the sky's soft blue ;
See why the bright stars twinkled, and if really
    The clouds were flocks of sheep,
With all his countless little footsteps weary,—
    Lay down and fell asleep.

'T was while the childish faith, in his small bosom,
    Was beautiful and bright,
In our good Saviour's story, and the legends
    Of holy Christmas night,
In that ethereal world of dream and fancy,
    O'er which kind fairies reign,
And in his power to stay, when he grew older,
    All sorrow, want, and pain.

Long will we miss thee, as we miss the sunbeams
    In autumn days ; thou wert
So mischievous and glad, so omnipresent
    In thy short, brown, checked skirt.
The block-house thou hadst built behind the wood-
        shed,
    Is out of all repair,
And when, with autumn days, the door creaks open,
    No roguish face is there.

Sometimes thy dimpled cheeks with clouds were
        shadowed,
    But only for a while,
The pout upon thy quivering lips relaxing,
    Would change into a smile ;
Then came the kiss of reconciliation,
    Thy small, choked breast would rise,
And then I 'd find what angels were, by looking
    In thy moist, loving eyes.

And every night, I 've drawn thy little playmates
    Upon my knee, and told
Them why thou layest, flower-strewn and small
        hands folded,
    So white, so still, so cold.
'T was but the preparation for the journey
    To a bright twinkling star,
Where a great King reigned, who sent forth each
        twelvemonth
    His angels near and far,—

To find and bring to live in his blest kingdom,
>The gentlest little child,
And this time, came the summons to their play-
>mate,
>So good, and pure and mild ;
And now they grieve no more, but think that some-
>time
>Their summons will be given,
And their small friend will come again and lead
>them
>Up the steep path to heaven.

THE UNKNOWABLE.

A PROBLEM strange is matter, for resolve it
o'er and o'er,
Into its simplest forms, we are no further than be-
fore ;
For then, a tiny grain, a germ invisible we hold,
Which still can be divided, though divided times
untold—
A grain which may become the air, the water, or
have power
To grow into a giant tree, or to a slender flower.

And what is motion ? who can tell whence comes
its secret force ?
Is it something ? is it nothing ? hath it end ? or
hath it source ?
The spirit of the earth and air, forward and backward tossed
From one thing to the other, never spent and never
lost ;

We see it in the growing grass, we hear it in the
    wind,
We seize it—it eludes our grasp, it will not be
    defined.

We cannot picture in the mind that kingdom vague
    called "space,"
For where there are no limits fixed, there is not any
    place ;
And pondering on this shadowy theme, the thought
    will rise that there
Must be, in all this dreary waste, a boundary fixed
    somewhere ;
Our refuge from that thought's to think that all the
    stars we see,
Compared with space, are as one hour in all eter-
    nity.

And when did time begin to reign ? and when will
    time be naught ?
That time is truly infinite, we cannot think the
    thought.
We 've said that time 's eternal, yet we know not
    what we say ;
The only image that can e'er the subtle truth con-
    vey
Is, that compared with time, the age which marks
    this planet's face
Is like our little universe, lost in the realms of
    space.

To these mysterious facts, all search must ulti-
mately tend,
And here, as 'gainst the solid rock, all thought and
quest must end ;
For we have found the infinite, that truth, so lightly
said,
Which from the grasp still soars, and leaves the
finite in its stead.
These strange, unknown realities must finally in-
still
Belief that they 're a part, a glimpse, of some almighty will ;
And so, at last, by matter, motion, space, and time,
we find
The impotence of human thought, the dearth of
human mind ;
And this dark veil before our eyes the best assur-
ance gives
That there must be a higher life and that the
eternal lives.

THE OLD SWING.

ROUND childhood's home I linger sadly,
    And note the changes time has made.
I watch the group of children playing,
    As once a little child I played,
With the old swing that still is hanging
    Beneath the giant elm-tree's shade.

And waiting till with twilight's coming
    The merry crowd departs—once more
I feel the old swing sway beneath me
    With mystic measure, as of yore.
Again I dream the dreams of boyhood,
    And live that sweet existence o'er.

It seems with every slow vibration,
    A magic pendulum of days,
Which backward moves, until my childhood
    Appears before my tear-dimmed gaze ;
And where the gray-haired man was dreaming,
    A careless, happy urchin sways.

He hears the rustling leaves and branches,
　The queer cicada's wizard tune.
He tries to solve the wondrous problems
　Of sky and earth, nor thinks how soon
In golden plans and childish fancies
　Will fade the smiling summer noon.

The child becomes the boyish dreamer,
　With future limitless and bright,
Outstretching to the land of fairies,
　Where he, a dauntless, loyal knight,
In search of some wronged, lovely princess,
　In the old swing takes many a flight.

Years pass : 't is dusk ; as by enchantment,
　The swing grows wide enough for two,
An ardent youth, a pretty maiden,
　Whom I in days long vanished knew,
That back and forth are slowly swaying,
　And talk in whispers faint and few.

Just then fate broke the link that bound me
　To that lost youth I loved so well,
And child and boy and lover faded
　And vanished with the broken spell.
For lo ! like all my airy castles,
　The old swing trembled, snapped, and fell.

WHEN THE HEAVENS WERE NEAR.

WHEN I was but a little boy,
   I thought that all that seemed was true,
All trivial things were springs of joy,
   The earth was glorious, bright and new.

The world was mine; 't was full, I thought,
   Of fairies, genii, rare delights
And palaces, by magic wrought;
   I 'd read it in the " Arabian Nights."

My faith was strong in Santa Claus,
   Whose gifts to good folks always came;
And now, I find far different laws
   Dividing honor, wealth and fame.

I thought that riches brought content,
   That friends were always true and kind,
With rainbows all the showers were blent,
   The clouds were always golden-lined.

The sloping hill, before our home,
  Seemed a steep, rugged mountain side ;
The small stream where we played, like some
  Historic river, deep and wide.

I thought the sky's blue crystal lay
  Just o'er the tree-tops on the hill ;
And now, heaven seems so far away,
  And every year grows farther still.

Years have crept by ; with silent grief,
  I 've seen each boyish hope decay,
Each bright conception and belief
  On life's stern river swept away.

Wealth, learning, aye ! the world I 'd give
  To be once more so near the sky,
Because, the longer that I live,
  The less, it seems, I 'm fit to die.

SHADOWS.

THE summer wind is sighing in the tree-tops,
    A melancholy tale;
The sparkling elm-leaves trace upon the heavens
    An ever-shifting veil.

The shadow of the chestnut moves and trembles
    Upon the waving grass,
The ripples of a sea of molten silver
    Along the meadow pass.

A cloud draws near—a ship with fleecy canvas.
    Its shadow o'er the lawn
Steals slowly on, like death, until the sunlight
    Fades, quivers—and is gone.

The rustic, ivied seat beneath the chestnut,
    Where often I have made
Her eyes grow moist, reading some quaint, sad story,
    Is lonely and decayed.

The morning-glory looks not in her window,
　　As once it used, to meet
The merry smile, which triumphed o'er the suffering
　　Of beauty pale and sweet.

We watched the solemn shadow nearer stealing,
　　Before the dark ship came,
And felt, that should a ray of sunlight follow,
　　'T would never be the same.

THE MAGIC MIRROR.

I.

'TWAS toward the close of a September day;
    The air was hazy; through a woodland screen,
Where sank the golden sun, a fiery ray
    Down slanting o'er the yellow, brown and green,
    Of corn, ploughed land and pasture, from the
        sheen
Of the broad Mohawk upward glanced again,
    And so enwrapt with flames incarnadine
A gabled mansion's windows, peaks, and vane,
That the old farm-house looked like castle built in
        Spain.

II.

Yet, with the sunset, it seemed lone and drear,
    For only lately, death had crossed the sill,
And since that morn, its mistress, Widow Vere,
    Slept in the little graveyard on the hill.
    Here, twenty years, she lived, proud, sad, and still,
With one old servant, since her child had fled
    With him she loved against the old dame's will;

And as she, too, for many years was dead,
A kinsman, far removed, the estate inherited.

III.

And he who now, long time with boisterous din,
   An entrance sought, was Winthrop Ford, the heir.
And when at last the door swung softly in,
   And no one came, as if a ghost were there,
   He entered through a hall-way, dim and square,
The musty regions of a darkened room,
   Where, hung on either wall, a cheerful care
Had worked a weeping willow and a tomb,
And framed two coffin-plates, to dissipate the
    gloom.

IV.

Thence gladly through the farther door his way
   He found into an oaken chamber ; here
Were portraits grave, a hearth and quaint display
   Of volumes, brown with dust of many a year,
   Chairs grimly carved, a sideboard dark and queer,
Whose glass gave back the sunset's dying flame ;
   And o'er the hearth he saw, pale, startling, near,
The likeness of a young and lovely dame,
Who seemed as if about to step down from the
    frame.

V.

She looked the heroine of some strange romance,
   And seemed to follow every move he made,
With a mysterious and disdainful glance,

Caught from old Colonel Vere, whose face, dis-
    played
With grim effect, above his trenchant blade
Of continental glory, Winthrop eyed
    With smile sarcastic, till, by beauty swayed,
He turned to her again, and petrified
With wonder, there beheld—a mirror, naught be-
    side.

VI.

Thence to an open window, with all speed,
    He sprang, but there no flying beauty found ;
Some clothes flapped on the line, an ancient steed,
    Like Pegasus, imprisoned in the pound,
    Gazed sadly o'er the fence, then turned around,
And eyed, with ludicrous surprise, the knight,
    Who ventured thus to tread enchanted ground.
A passage, then, whose door stood opposite
The mirror, gave a clue to that fair vision's flight.

VII.

And in its darkness, venturing to explore,
    He reached the attic stairs, then turned aside
And found his way unto another door,
    Which, as he came, creaked loud and opened
        wide
Upon the castle kitchen, where he spied
An ancient crone, who, if she were in truth
    The enchanted fair,—was much transmogrified,
And who supposed, a fairy prince, forsooth,
This apparition swift, of such tall, handsome
    youth.

VIII.

But, when her fright allowed him to explain,
  The rightful heir, with stately courtesy,
She welcomed, like some feudal castelaine,
  And forthwith darted out and speedily
    Brought the "baked funeral meats," which
      proved to be
Cheese, doughnuts and mince pie, a goodly cheer;
  Then, while he ate, traced out the family tree
In all its branches, from its earliest year,
And told him many a tale of proud old Madame
    Vere.

IX.

The supper ended, by a fire which blazed
  Upon the hearth, for now the nights were cold,
He sat and smoked, and in the mirror gazed,
  Hoping that there, once more, he might behold
  That ghostly girl, of such enchanting mould,
Whose beauty, subtile as some faint perfume,
  Filled him with fancies, strange and manifold.
And now the twilight deepened into gloom,
The fire had burned low down, and darkness filled
    the room.

X.

An influence supernatural seemed to fill
  The strange old mansion, even the doors had
    caught
The charm, and opened of their own sweet will,
  And all things were with that bright vision
    fraught,

That face, of which it seemed he 'd always thought.
Then, suddenly, the wood blazed up once more,
   Lighting the room ; his eyes the mirror sought,
And there he saw, within the passage door,
The enchanted princess stand, pale, mystic as
      before.

XI.

Her face was oval and her figure tall ;
   Her hair, with silver comb of quaint device,
Flowed waving from a fair, low brow, to fall
   Upon a small, round neck ; the sweet surprise
   Of parted lips, arched piquantly ; large gray eyes,
Mysterious in the dancing light ; and then
   A dimpled chin, softened what otherwise
A too disdainful beauty would have been ;—
This much he saw before the blaze died out again.

XII.

Then springing up, he struck a light and found
   The open door ; a gust thence sweeping blew
The light out ; something rustled ; with a bound
   He rushed into the passage, stumbled through,
   And up the stairway to the attic flew.
A phantom shape before the window crossed,
   And falling o'er a spinning-wheel or two,
He grasped a fluttering garment, but the ghost
Changed to an old silk gown upon a rafter tossed.

XIII.

He stretched his length before the hearth again,
   And, watching by a lamplight's flickering gleam,

Thought surely that the colonel winked, and then
    He slept and dreamed a most unheard-of dream :
    Goblins and spooks swept by in motley stream ;
And then 't was changed, and the enchanted fair
    Sat sleeping by the hearth, while what would seem
The ghost of Madame Vere, with silvery hair,
Stooped down, and in her face peered with a
    ghastly stare.

XIV.

To shield such sleeping loveliness from harm,
    For 'neath the spell she moved with many a sigh ;
He strove, but could not stir, to break the charm,
    Until, the rusty sword, which dangled nigh,
    Perceiving, in the twinkling of an eye
He seized, and at the ghost, with all his will,
    Flung it, and presto ! wakened instantly
By a great fall of glass,—with sudden thrill
He saw the face once more the magic mirror fill.

XV.

But now, behold ! her look, her garb portrayed
    A curious change, as if in antique dress,
She were bedizened for a masquerade,
    While in her hair, the silver comb, no less,
    Smacked of the days of some dead ancestress,
Then to a door, which opened opposite,
    He turned, and saw—no dream of loveliness,
But the old servant, robed in ghostly white,
Who spoke of direful sounds and trembled with
    affright.

XVI.

He pointed at the vision ; drawing near,
  She cried : " The missus' portrait ! yes ! 't is she ;
Took, when she scarce was twenty, many a year,
  Because it pained her lonely heart to see
  Her face so gay and handsome, and to free
Her saintly mind from worldly thoughts and cares,
  'T was covered by a mirror, goodness me !
Who broke it ? I was frightened from my prayers
And then, an hour ago, sech fearful sounds up-
    stairs !

XVII.

" Jest after Hilda Gaylord came to change
  The book she borrowed as you came."   " And
    pray !
Who is this Hilda ? " 'T was a story strange
  The old dame told ; how Hilda came one day
  Like princess of a fairy tale, to stay
At Neighbor Crain's ; this princess fair, 't was true,
  Taught in the village school, across the way,
And oft had sat and watched the whole night
    through
With Madam Vere. But whence she came, no
  mortal knew.

XVIII.

" You ought to see her.   Why ! she looks,—well
    there !
  It 's curious that I never thought so, jest
Exactly like that picture ; I declare !

If Hester Vere, who died away out West,
    Had had a child—I 'd think—well now, I 'm
        blest !
Some say she had, and then, her age, jest right
    For Hilda, and, what 's stranger than the rest,
The missus called her Hester Vere, one night.
My sakes ! it 's all so plain, right out in black and
        white."

XIX.

The truth was out, and Hilda proved next day
    To be the dame's granddaughter ; naught was
        clearer,
And yet the enchantment ceased not, strange to
        say ;
    He found her daily lovelier and dearer,
    And blest his luck, for if, with tastes austerer,
He had not supped so well, and in a trance
    Levelled the poker at the magic mirror,—
He had forever lost the golden chance,
And Hilda had not been the mistress of the
        manse.

THALIA.

OFTEN, when the hearth fire smoulders,
    In the evening's deepening gloom,
There has stol'n a ghostly maiden
    To my lonely, haunted room,
    And dispelled the doubt and gloom.

At my feet she sits and looks up
    With those great dark eyes at me,
With a glance now grave, now roguish,
    With her white arms on my knee,
    Childlike, she looks up to me.

And she tells me weighty secrets
    Of the fairies, of the elves,
Till the embers, till the grotesque
    Porcelain figures on the shelves,
    Take the forms of dancing elves.

Through the growing darkness steals a
    Perfume faint from fairy-land,

And I feel her round arms' pressure,
　　Feel her brown hair brush my hand,
　　Think that I 'm in fairy-land.

Then we talk of times long vanished,
　　Talk of many a boyish dream,
Weave, of long-departed fancies,
　　Chains that bright and fragile seem
　　As a child's glad golden dream.

Each day, deeper still and clearer,
　　I have read in her dark eyes
Romances of love and fancy,
　　Till my very being lies
　　In those ghostly, glorious eyes.

And though I have known and loved her
　　For these many weary years,
Every day, more sweet and childlike,
　　Her pale oval face appears,
　　For these many long, long years

CHRISTMAS.

WEARY were the days of autumn,
  Long and cold the nights of winter,
And our hearts were colder still ;
We had drained the cup of sorrow,
Wandered through the shadowy valley,
  Bowed before the Almighty will.

Grief had grown subdued and holy,
For we knew we had a treasure
  In that home, so far away,
Had a little intercessor,
An ambassador in heaven,
  Waiting for us night and day.

By the hearth we sat in darkness,
With a little chair between us,
  As we sat a year before,
When we listened for the reindeer's

Tinkling bells, and told the many
  Wondrous things of Christmas lore,—

Sat as when he last was with us ;
Thus, our sad imaginations
  Would a quaint deception weave,
And our strange and mournful fancy
Try to conjure back his presence
  On that lonely Christmas eve.

And the time wore on, till, startled
From my reveries by the pressure
  Of a soft and childish hand,
Lo ! I saw, between us sitting,
Just as though he ne'er had journeyed
  To that unknown far-off land,

Golden-haired, brown-eyed, and dimpled,
Listening, wondering, and expectant,
  Once again,—our little child.
But the guileless face was brighter
With the joy of the immortals,
  With a radiance sweet and mild.

Thus, the second time, from heaven,
Like the Christ-child, with a Christmas
  Gift of gladness, he has come ;
And, invisible to others,
With his little hands he leads us
  Daily, hourly, nearer home.

And his silent, radiant presence
Teaches patience, resignation,
   Makes the dark ways bright and plain,
Calms our hearts and makes us tender
For all sorrow, want, and suffering,
   Makes us children once again.

MY NOVEL.

I WILL write some time a novel,
  Simple, thrilling and romantic ;
Beautiful shall be the heroine,
Very beautiful and tender.

Artfully will I arrange it,
And contrive to paint her portrait,
So that she I love will know it
Instantly for her own picture.

Almost black shall be her eyebrows
And her hair's rich wavy masses,
But her eyes, large, star-like, dreamy,
Bluer than the sky at midnight.

Rosy tints, like morn and evening,
O'er her cheek shall steal and vanish ;
Round her mouth a smile shall linger,
And her chin shall have a dimple.

Every gesture, every outline
Of the slender, rounded figure;
Every gay or sad expression,
Floating o'er the lovely features,

Shall suggest some rare old painting;
Shall suggest some sweet, quaint poem;
On the heart shall leave an imprint
That shall never be forgotten.

Almost, yet not quite, a goddess;
Sometimes haughty, sometimes roguish;
Just enough of faults I 'll give her
So that one may dare to love her.

And the youth who loves this maiden,
From the day he first beholds her,
Shall be learned, grave and thoughtful,
Sad, poetical and silent.

After sighing long in secret,
He shall write a tender romance,
Wherein he will be the lover,
She will be the pretty heroine.

In this romance, all the long years
Of his sighing will be numbered;
In this romance there will happen
All the scenes that he has pictured.

When, from some impending danger,
In the mountains, on the sea-shore,

From the flood, or fire, the lover
Risks his life to save his mistress,—

She will find, at last, she loves him,
And contrive some way to say so ;
Perhaps by sending him an envied
Bunch of violets from her bosom.

Thus, the hero and the heroine
He shall paint with such true colors,
That she cannot help but see it ;
Cannot help but know his secret.

And her gentle heart, beleaguered
By a love so full of fancy,
And so delicate and constant,
Shall surrender all its treasures.

In her voice and in the shadows
Of her eyes and in her blushes,
He shall read the story plainly,
And behold ! my novel 's written.

MIDNIGHT.

THERE 'S a time at night, when quickly
　　The blue of the sky grows dark,
Hushed is the cricket's chirping,
　　Vanished the fire-fly's spark.

The trees are great black giants,
　　Cloaked, and silent, and tall ;
Each star 's a glittering diamond,
　　Each cloud 's a jet-black pall.

There 's a stir in the solemn darkness,
　　As of a wind in the trees,
As of a brook's low rustle,—
　　But 't is not the stream or breeze.

It swells, like the murmur of tempests,
　　Then lessens and sinks away,
As if 't were the winging up of the souls
　　Of those who had died in the day.

Though the world is hid in darkness,
  In my life 's a calm bright light,
In the quietness of that moment,
  Which comes at the dead of night.

Then I see though the doubts which beset me,
  As I never before have done,
And regrets and fierce ambitions
  Fade slowly, one by one.

THE GAME OF CHESS.

'TWAS stinging, blustering winter weather,
　　How well I recollect the night !
When Kate and I played chess together.
　　Her beauty in the hearth-fire's light
Seemed more Madonna-like and rosy ;
The hours were swift, the room was cosy,
　　The windows frosted, silvery white.

Even now I see that grave face resting
　　Upon the hand, so white and small ;
I see that mystic grace, suggesting
　　A painter's dream ; I oft recall
Her glance, now anxious, gay, or tender ;
The girlish form, complete yet slender,
　　In silhouette against the wall.

It was not strange that I was mated,
　　For 't was my fondly cherished aim.
I longed to speak, but I was fated,
　　The rightful opening never came.
I pawned my heart for her sweet favor,

With every look, some vantage gave her,
   And so, alas ! I lost the game.

Since then, by fortune, love, forsaken,
   Through checkered years I 've passed and seen
My castles fall, my pawns all taken,
   My spotless knights prove traitors mean ;
And worn, with many a check, I wander
Like the poor vanquished king, and ponder
   With sadness on my long-lost queen.

PAQUITA.

I.

IT was night, and we were anchored,
  Off the town of Fernandina ;
Miles above, we saw the beacon
Shine from old Ramiro's landing
Like a star, across the water ;
And up spoke the captain, saying :

II.

" I have seen the fair Paquita,
She who came, enthralled and left us,
At St. Augustine, last winter ;
I have braved the fierce old Argus,
Braved the anger of Ramiro,
I have come and seen and conquered."

III.

Then with tone and laugh derisive,
Answered, straightway, Randolph Gordon :
" You are still, an empty boaster.

I, myself, have seen Paquita,
And the month shall scarce have ended,
Ere I ask you to our wedding."

IV.

While they spoke I sat in silence,
Though my heart was strangely tortured,
For I, too, had known Paquita,
When she came to St. Augustine,
And her face rose up before me,
Dark and sad, with eyes love lighted,

V.

As she looked, when last we parted,
When she promised to remember.
"Their's," thought I, "are idle vauntings;
I myself will seek Ramiro's,
And Paquita, she shall tell me
If 't was all an idle fancy."

VI.

Night, once more, the earth had mantled,
As I sat with Don Ramiro,
'Neath Ramiro's broad piazza,
While his daughter, light as Hebe,
Came and vanished, bringing Reinas,
Bringing Cognac or Marsala.

VII.

In her dark, sweet face, I vainly
Sought a look of recognition.

She was cold and strange and silent,
Just as beautiful as ever,
But she did not seem as tender,
Did not seem the same Paquita.

VIII.

But when darker grew the garden,
And Ramiro's red cigar light
Seemed the one eye of an ogre,
Some one stole and stood beside me,
Some one whispered "I remember,"
Pressed my hand and turned and left me.

IX.

As I rose to seek the landing,
From Ramiro's house departing,
Came the sound of whispering voices,
Came the sound of girlish laughter.
"Surely! there is some strange secret
In this household of the Spaniard."

X.

As I watched Ramiro's beacon,
On my way across the water,
All at once it paled and vanished.
When I came on deck the captain
Had departed, none knew whither.
'T was a night of strange surprises—

XI.

Strange surprises, never ending,
For at dawn 't was found that Gordon,

In some curious way, had vanished.
That day passed, another followed,
And at night there came two letters—
This is what the captain wrote me :

XII.

"Love has triumphed, Will ! *Paquita
Fled last night with me to Charleston.*
Old Ramiro would have killed her,
So she said, if he had caught us.
Please inform the proud Castilian,
And condole with Randolph Gordon."

XIII.

Gordon wrote me, from Savannah :
"Will ! *Paquita 's mine ; we came here
On the boat which leaves at midnight.*
How she loved me ! how she trembled !
Lest our flight should rouse Ramiro ;—
I 'm so sorry for the captain."

XIV.

Rage, despair, and doubt possessed me
At these tidings, so conflicting.
Were there, really, two Paquitas ?
Was my love returned by neither ?
With these tidings, to Ramiro,
With these letters, straight I hastened.

XV.

Loud and long laughed Don Ramiro,—
Laughed until his face grew purple ;

In the door-way something rustled,
And I looked and saw—Paquita ;
Saw her standing, like a statue,
With a statue's rounded outlines.

XVI.

In the shadows and the dimples
Of her face a strange smile lingered,
And a roguish light came dancing
In her eyes' unfathomed darkness ;
Like a sweet, embodied riddle,
Mystic, fanciful, she stood there.

XVII.

Speech came back to Don Ramiro—
Speech came back, though slow and broken :
"With the captain fled Aurora ;
Inez, now, is Madam Gordon ;
Was it not the poor old father
Got them ready for the journey ?

XVIII.

They not know I have three daughters—
Yes ! Señor ! born all the same time.
It is twins ? no ? what you call them ?
And Paquita 's all that 's left me.
She, Señor ! will make the best wife ;
You can have her, if you want her."

MENDELSSOHN'S "LIEDER OHNE WORTE."

I

SWEET SOUVENIR.

'TIS nothing but a picture
   With outlines dim and faint,
A picture of a young girl, dressed
   In fashion old and quaint.
In that picture there are graces
   An artist could not paint,
And a face, the fairest, loveliest,
   E'er possessed by girl or saint.

In that face there is the tenderest
   Look that maiden ever wore ;
In that look there 's something tells me
   Of the golden days of yore.
In those days there was a story,
   Would that I could live it o'er !
The story of the passionate love
   I cherish evermore.

7

CONTEMPLATION.

At midnight, by the window,
　　I sat, till all was still,
Then pictured her before me
　　By passionate strength of will.

I weighed each trait of her beauty,
　　Each charm of mind and soul,
Till I conjured her before me
　　In one sweet, life-like whole.

With that dreamy look I loved so,
　　She stood in the shadowy light,
Pale and still as a lily
　　Alone in a garden at night.

Her look was kind and tender,
　　I never had seen her so.
She loved me, this dream maiden loved me,
　　Though the other was cold as snow.

44

LOOKING BACK.

I 've gained the mountain top, and turning,
　　Look with tearful gaze
　　On the path which brings me
　　Back to childhood's days.

Childish mountains, like my childish troubles,
    Dwarf and sink from view ;
    Youth's brightest scenes have somehow
    Lost their golden hue.

Graves of all my hopes and fond ambitions
    Dead so long ago,—
    All my wandering, weary footsteps
    Mark the vale below.

And, looking back with sad composure,
    On the path of years,
    I am calmer for those vanished tempests,
    Happier for my tears.

A CASTLE IN NEW ENGLAND.

UPON the torrent's brink, there stands
    A castle, gray and old,
With drawbridge, barbican and keep,
    With turrets manifold,
And banners, floating in the sun,
    Like bands of burnished gold.

High up, above the grated arch,
    The embrasured casements frown ;
And there, a ladye young and fair,
    For many a day looks down
The roadway, winding o'er the bridge
    Into the ancient town.

Upon the fields of waving grain,
    Her mournful glances rest ;
She watches every cloud that floats
    Beyond the hill's blue crest ;
Until, at last, an armored knight
    Rides down, from out the west.

The vision fades, the scene is changed,
  In one swift, magic whirl ;
A homely, gabled house succeeds
  This castle of an earl ;
The princess in the tower becomes
  A fair New England girl.

She sits beneath the porch at eve,
  The time unreckoned flies,
Her little hands are clasped, her book,
  Unread, before her lies ;
A fanciful and far-off look
  Is in her tender eyes.

Across her faintly dimpled cheeks
  The lights and shadows glance,
Her sweet and thoughtful face is raised,
  She seems as in a trance,
There is an aureole round her head
  Of glory and romance.

And this was all a dream of hers,
  Her thought's fantastic flight ;
A dream which changed her homely house
  Into a castle bright ;
A dream which made of farmer Brown
  A handsome, armored knight.

By homely tasks and trivial cares
  Her life is compassed round ;

Her dreamy knowledge of the world
  In quaint old books is found ;
Beyond those blue New England hills
  'T is all an unknown ground.

Yet often, in the air, a strange,
  Mysterious music seems ;
Old towns and lordly castles rise
  In her romantic dreams ;
The glow of knighthood's golden days
  Across her pathway streams.

While there are maids so sweet, shall fame
  Of deeds chivalric fade ?
Come forth ! O knight ! upon whose shield
  There is no spot or shade,
And lay your lance in rest, to win
  This fair New England maid !

THE LAST DAY OF SUMMER.

EACH day more bright, each day with softer
    glow,
  At dawn and eve ; the summer time has passed
Like a long, pleasant revery and lo !
  This day has come, the loveliest and the last.

Woods, meadows, corn-fields are like chequered
    squares,
  Painted in various colors, bright and gay.
Summer, as with a mournful fancy, wears
  Her richest garments, e'er she fades away.

The soft, clear light's enchantment makes the chain
  Of distant hills seem strangely near at hand,
And gives to well-known scenes and objects plain
  The glamour and the charm of fairyland.

A few white clouds, in shapes fantastic, rise
  Above the woods, which crest the highest hill ;
'T is like the landscape of a dream, it lies
  So deeply calm, so wonderfully still.

And there are other clouds and hills and woods,
  In the smooth mirror of the lazy stream ;
Vague, unattainable, shadowy solitudes
  Of lotus land, a dream within a dream.

There 's naught in motion, save the quaint balloon
  Of thistle-down ; there is no hum of bees ;
There 's something ghostly in the cricket's tune,
  The cobwebbed hedge, the shadows of the trees

The winding brook is choked and half concealed
  By clumps of cat-tails and of golden-rod ;
The cattle, grazing in the far-off field,
  Are still as figures in the land of Nod.

The air is filled with something sweet and strange,
  And nature seems to pause and hold her breath,
Before this sign of an impending change,
  This deep, mysterious calm, which heralds death.

And now, the wondrous work of nature ends ;
  Now, is its glorious fulness manifest
In this last, quiet summer's day, which blends
  A solemn beauty and a perfect rest.

THE SISTERS.

IN the long night's lonely musing,
  Comes the vision of two sisters
That I loved in days long vanished—
Loved, yet knew not which I loved most.

One was rosy, fair, and dimpled,
Romping, laughing, dreaming, sighing ;
By her roguish glance enchanted,
Queen of all my thoughts, I owned her.

Dark and mystic was the other,
Dark and sad and meditative ;
When her eyes grew soft and tender,
She it was who seemed the dearest.

Years have past since we were parted
By the bitter tongues of envy ;
Many years, and many changes,
Like an ocean lie between us.

But their looks of kindly interest,
Patience, virtues, tears, and laughter,
Words of cheer and praise and comfort,
Gentle ways and sweet refinements,

Like the stars of night, have lighted
Me along the world's dark pathway ;
Like the hands of fairies, shortened
My apprenticeship in manhood.

And I weave this little chaplet
Of the flowers of love and romance,
For those gentle sisters, long since
Sleeping in the silent city.

THE OCEAN.

LONG I watched the ocean, with its mournful, never
  Ceasing tide, each ship, that from the horizon stole,
  Floated by, grew less and vanished, seemed a soul,
That upon the years, from some far shadowy river,
Slowly steals, until, with sail of strong endeavor,
  Hope and yearning, it sweeps by unto its goal,
  Fades and sinks into oblivion, while the roll
Of the solemn flood of years goes on forever.
Now the darkness hides the ocean and the shore,
  And the ships have long since vanished in the distance,
Yet I hear the breakers' dull, monotonous roar
  Tell the story o'er again, with strange insistance,—
Hear the ancient ocean's hoarse voice evermore
  Chant the mystic, sad refrain of man's existence.

THE RIVER.

OFT have I watched the sunset's mellow light,
   That through the window streams upon the
     wall,
   Like a mysterious river, rise and fall.
The lengthening shadows deepen into night,
And still, as if a part indefinite,
   Of life and time and hope, a part of all
   The thoughts and scenes and joys that I recall,
Thou flowest on, O river deep and bright!
And I must watch, without the power to stay,
   Thy tide that surges on resistlessly,
Thy dancing waves that bear the years away.
   O thou relentless flood! give back to me,
The life, that on thy current, day by day,
   Is floating, floating, floating to the sea!

THE CASTLE BY THE SEA.

A CASTLED crag, half hidden in a wreath
 Of ocean mist, an eagle's circling flight,
The little islands, reefs and breakers white
Of a broad sea, whose waters dash and seethe
Against the rock, a thousand feet beneath,
 The sudden gleaming of a beacon light
 From the old tower upon the crag, when night
His gloomy shadow o'er the earth doth breathe,
And answering watch fires, blazing near and far
 From every headland,—all that I have told,
And more, in evening sky and cloud and star,
 Pictured above the horizon, I behold,
And magic scenes create, that changeful are,
 As those same hues of crimson and of gold.

THE MOHAWK VALLEY, FROM RICH-FIELD HILL.

I CLIMBED a winding roadway to the brim
  Of a gigantic basin, walled around
   With hills and hills and hills, whose tops were
    crowned
With forest dense, and whose remotest rim,
Gorge seamed, through summer haze looked blue
    and dim.
   Far down a lazy snake-like river wound,
   And all was silence, perfect and profound.
I saw the white clouds' shadows slowly skim
O'er meadows, cornfields, woods, as bright and
    still
   As painted squares, the bluest dome expand
From ridge to ridge, and 'neath a sheltering hill
   The whitest, smallest, sleepiest hamlet stand.
Surely ! the world's fierce tide ne'er rose, until
   It stole within this dreamy wonderland.

THE GORGE.

BEFORE me, standing at the craggy head
   Of a great gorge, the wildest, loveliest scene
  Of nature lies : far down in the ravine,
Choked with great hemlocks, and the yellow and
    red
Of birch and maple, like a silver thread,
   A small stream winds and widens to the sheen
  Of a blue lake, that, glassy and serene
With distance, at the gorge's mouth is spread ;
Marked with white farm-house and tree-tufted hill,
   For miles beyond, fields ploughed and green
     extend,
Even to the horizon's edge, until
   Like pleasant thought, that in a dream doth end,
The vista, grown more faint and soft and still,
   Its hues, at length, with heaven's pale gray doth
     blend.

TWILIGHT.

MAIDEN ! who veiled in robes of sombre shade
    Dost haunt the glen and through the forest
      roam,
  What time the clouds float o'er the heaven's blue
      dome,
In changing, fading, glorious hues arrayed—
Art thou, indeed, a sad and lovelorn maid,
  Or shy and gentle spirit, who doth come
  Each day, at evening, from her mossy home,
Some grotto, hidden 'neath a wild cascade?
I seek thee many times, and suddenly,
  When the bright tints have died out from the
      west,
With sweet, pale face, as in a revery,
  Passes the gray-eyed maiden of my quest.
Through copse, through glen, in vain I follow thee,
  The first star twinkles and thou vanishest.

THE FOUNTAIN.

THE fountain's crystal depths contain
   For thee, O maiden ! fair as shy,
  A realm of fairy mystery,
For there, enchanted, long hath lain
A strange and beautiful domain.
  Look down upon its trees and sky,
  Its towers, its white clouds floating by,
As through some wizard's window pane !
And lo ! even now, a princess fair
  Gazed from those depths, as if she might
Enchanted be, awaiting there
  The coming of the valiant knight,
Who seeketh always, everywhere,
  To aid and succor beauty bright.

THE SHELL.

WITH wonder great, I heard a small voice say,
　　From the deep coral chamber of a shell :
"A woful maid am I, of those that dwell
Beneath the sea ; a curious power have they,
To walk as spirits ; while I thus did stray
　　It stormed, and I in deepest slumber fell
　　Within this hollow, many-tinted shell,
Which, when I woke, upon the sea-beach lay.
Because a prisoner I must be, until
　　Within the ocean's depths, there, I entreat
That thou return the shell, and often will
　　I cause large pearls to glisten at thy feet,
And o'er the waves' sad music sound, and fill
　　Thy dreams with maidens' faces, pale and sweet."

VALESKA.

VALESKA ! fair unknown ! whose portrait graces
   The old oak room,—what fancies strange arise
  At thy slight figure's antiquated guise,
Thy white, round neck half hid in dainty laces,
And palest, dreamiest, ghostliest of faces !
  I love thee, for the tender thought that lies
  In the sweet shadows of thy hazel eyes,
And on thy lips, in mournful, lingering traces.
At night, I gaze upon thy beauty, quaintly
   Glowing above the hearth-fire's ruddy flame,
Until the hour when, queen-like, sad and saintly,
   Thou stepp'st down from thy portrait ; thy dear
      name
I speak—and starting, see thee, smiling faintly
  A mystic smile, fade back into the frame.

DUSK.

WE are all here again, in the twilight:
   The dark, swaying trees and the sky,
The wanderer wind and the ivy,
   The clouds that sail up and float by,
   The flowers, the grass and I.

The shadows grow broader and deeper,
   I hear the wandering breeze
Rustling up in the branches
   And telling the solemn trees,
   Of prairies and of seas.

And a vision strange steals upon me,
   In that changing fanciful light,
A small apparition comes, chasing
   A moth in its zigzag flight—
   'T is a little child, in white.

In the swing, 'neath the giant elm-tree,
   He slowly sways to and fro,

Lost in a day-dream and wondering
  If the full, white clouds are snow,
  And what makes the fire-flies glow.

The picture has long since vanished
  In the gloom of an evening mild,
Yet still in the past I linger,
  With thoughts of those days beguiled,
  When I was that little child.

THE WIND IN THE TREES.

IN the night I lie by the window,
 And hear the wind in the trees,
And give to its ceaseless rustling
 And sighing, what meaning I please.

At first, 't is the wash of the ocean
 On a rugged, desolate shore ;
Or a fire on the hearth, in winter,
 Beginning to flicker and roar.

'T is a waterfall, in the distance,
 Whose cadence floats to the ear,
Now a far off, indistinct murmur,
 Now thundering, loud and clear.

'T is some giant, imprisoned spirit,
 Who groans and struggles in vain,
Writhing up in his anguish,
 Then sinking to earth again.

'T is the endless war for existence,
  Waged by the hosts of mankind,
Now the battle's rush sways toward me,
  Now it dies away on the wind.

And, at last, 't is the conflict within me,
  Of thoughts that will never cease,
Till the dawn looks gray through the tree tops,
  And the night winds sink in peace.

Thus long in the night, I listen
  To this strangest of symphonies,
This music, so quaint and solemn,
  The sound of the wind in the trees.

THE OAK WOOD.

I WANDERED through a holy, gloomy
   Oak wood, where 'neath violets wild
A brooklet murmured softly, faintly,
   As the praying of a child.

There fell a shadowy dread upon me,
   There came a rustling strange and low,
As if the wood might tell me something,
   That yet my heart was not to know.

As if to me it might discover
   Some secret of God's mystic will,
Then seemed it suddenly to tremble
   Before God's presence and was still.

JOHN WENTWORTH'S WILL.

I.

EACH breaker rolled in, like a smooth green
    wall,
  With crest o'er curling as it neared the land,
Where into foam it dashed with deafening brawl
  At Philip's feet : yet he, of ocean's grand
And melancholy voice, unconscious all,
  Gazed downward fixedly upon the sand ;
For airy footprints, small beyond compare,
Proved that some graceful nymph had wandered
    there.

II.

Along a wild shore, full of lonely charms,
  These traces following, he found at last
A nook fantastic, hollowed by the storms,
  Where, in the shadow of a stranded mast,
Her brown hair half concealing her round arms,
  With book clasped in her hands, lay sleeping fast,
Like that famed princess of the days of old,
A maiden of fair face and gentle mold.

III.

As he beheld the dark, fantastic face,
　There rose the fabric of a strange romance.
She seemed the daughter of some Eastern race—
　A Spanish maid,—by some mysterious chance
Here shipwrecked ; for a nameless foreign grace
　Hung like a dream upon her gentle trance,
And clothed with magic charm from head to feet
The girlish figure, slender, yet complete.

IV.

Long time he gazed, then stole with noiseless
　　tread
　From that enchanted scene of fairy-land,
Not knowing that, had he but turned his head,
　He would have seen her dark eyes wide expand,
And fill with roguish sunbeams as she read
　These lines, which he had traced upon the sand :
"Fair dreamer ! know that a poor youth this day
Gazed on thy face, and loved, and passed away ! "

V.

Time fled ; once more he came, aye ! many a day
　He wandered by the sea, but 't was in vain.
A sweet illusion, she had passed away ;
　And like an airy dream, came not again.
Time passed ; the earth with autumn tints was gay,
　And in a rumbling, hurrying railway train,
Past pleasant vales, blue hills, and forests dun,
All day he journeyed toward the setting sun.

VI.

'T was dark, when to a stage-coach queer and old
 He changed, for he must travel all night still
Across a mountain roadway, to behold
 His future bride ; for, by a curious will,
His Uncle John had left his long-saved gold
 And goodly lands in trust for him, until—
Condition strange, of a most strange bequest,—
He married Marcia Brown, some girl out West.

VII.

The coach rolled on, and with a heart like lead,
 He saw, in fancy, his prospective bride,
Some awkward country girl, and wished instead
 'T were that fair dreamer by the whispering tide,
Who from his quest to shadowy realms had fled.
 A few stars twinkled on his lonely ride ;
The village lights, like dancing fire-flies, winked,
And woods and fences grew more indistinct.

VIII.

The mantled figure of the traveller strange,
 Who shared his ride, had faded from his view ;
His thoughts assumed a more fantastic range ;
 'T was fairy-land ; a courser, good and true,
The stage-coach had become with magic change ;
 The princess had been found, and wakened
  through
A loving kiss ; and he, the lucky knight,
Was bearing his fair prize to realms of light.

IX.

He woke, upstarting, at his journey's goal,
  And found the stranger gone, the morning gray.
From a small nosegay in his button-hole
  There came a perfume faint, and, strange to say,
Around the flowers, traced on a crumpled scroll,
  These foolish lines of his had found their way :
" Fair dreamer ! know that a poor maid this day
Gazed on thy face, and loved, and passed away."

X.

He sat upon the porch with Geoffrey Brown ;
  It was a square brick house of days gone by,
And faced the river, toward whose banks sloped
     down
  The checkered squares of meadow, corn, and rye ;
And while they talked of changes in the town,
  Of prices, politics, demand, supply,
Philip thought sadly of the startled dame,
Who vanished in the kitchen as he came.

XI.

Then to that romance by the lonely shore
  Of ocean his sad fancy turned again,
And to his curious ride the night before
  With that strange voyager, who must have been
His fairy princess, found and lost once more ;
  Flown like a dream, he knew not where or when ;
And all the time old Geoffrey talked away,
And told what crops did best in sand or clay,—

XII.

Told, while it seemed a changeless, far-off hum,
  How he and Wentworth went to school together ;
Talked of his short-horn cattle, and of some
  Uninteresting lawsuit, of the weather,
And lastly of his Marcia, who had come
  From visiting "way down East"; she was
      "rather"
The smartest, prettiest lady ever seen,
And cooked, spoke French, and warbled like a
      queen.

XIII.

He soon should see her ; just then, on the stair,
  Philip heard light, quick footsteps coming down,
And all at once beheld a vision rare,
  And saw his princess change to Marcia Brown ;
Her face, resplendent, sweet beyond compare,
  Had not the slightest shadow of a frown ;
And so it came that Philip did fulfil
The strange conditions of "John Wentworth's
      will."

A PANTOMIME.

CIRCLED by a laughing, chattering,
  Merry group of little girls,
Like a rose girt round with pansies,
  Or a sapphire set with pearls,
He beheld her at the children's
  Pantomime on Christmas night,
Radiant, queen-like, 'neath the magic
  Of the music and the light,
  On a frosty winter's night.

Harlequin and Columbine
  Phantoms seemed, from fairy-land ;
But the clown, the wond'rous Guido,
  Changed all things with swift command
Into laughter, as a wizard's
  Touch turns every thing to gold.
She, alone, amid the laughing
  Throng, sat silent, pale and cold,
  Like some portrait framed in gold.

From that hour a glorious vision
  Haunted him by night and day ;
Never from his fancy vanished
  That pale face, those eyes of gray.
Round her home he often lingered,
  In the twilight's deepening gloom,
Watching till the slender shadow,
  'Gainst the curtain of her room,
  Should dispel the doubt and gloom.

Till the spring and summer faded,
  And the autumn's richness passed,
And to her enchanting presence
  He had found his way at last.
Those were glimpses into heaven,
  Those short hours that flew so fast,
'T was a strange, idyllic romance,
  Far too bright, too sweet to last.

All his hopes and dreams he told her,
  While her gentle heart forgave
That he gazed so long and fondly
  At her beauty pale and grave.
But at night the spell was ended ;
  From her side he must away ;
To some strange toil he was fated,
  What it was he might not say,—
  Sad and silent, stole away.

Winter came ; once more her presence
  Graced the Christmas pantomime ;

Ne'er before had scenes so golden
　　Been since old Arcadian time.
But the clown, the wond'rous Guido,
　　When the mimic play was done,
As he bowed before the foot-lights,
　　Seemed the prince of smiles and fun—
　　But the pantomime was done.

And he suddenly looked upward,
　　And his eyes met hers by chance,
'Neath the painted mask were features
　　She knew well ; a long, long glance,
Full of grave surprise and pity,
　　Sad, yet cold, she gave the clown ;
And he saw love's long-wrought fabric
　　Tremble, crack, and tumble down,—
　　Saw she ne'er could love the clown.

JACK'S LETTER TO BOB.

D EAR Bob ! I am going to be married.
  But before saying more, I must write
About something which weighs on my conscience.
  Of course, you remember that night,
In the carnival season at Venice,
  When we trained through that dampest of towns,
With that party of jolly Venetians,
  That at first we mistook for the Browns ?

How, after the ball, I was married,
  In joke, to an angel in black ?
To that ghostly and dark-haired Marchesa,
  The madcap queen of the pack ?
Her mask simply heightened the romance,
  And the joke seemed immense, till I knew
That that rascally priest was a real one,
  Which made me uncommonly blue.

For they said that the marriage was legal,
  And things took a serious shape,

Till you got up a duel and killed me,
    To get me out of the scrape,
And I took the next steamer for Naples,
    And left my fair widow to fate ;—
It 's queer how her eyes come and haunt me,
    Whenever I 'm thinking of Kate.

I could kick myself well, when I think that
    I played such an asinine rôle,
And I pray that you 'll bury the secret
    Deep down in your innermost soul,
For my Kate would make things rather lively
    For me, if she ever found out.
And now I will tell in what manner
    Our little affair came about.

We met on the steamer from Naples,
    Whence I sailed, as you know, for the States,
And at table kind fortune had placed me
    In the chair which was opposite Kate's.
She 's a friend of the Browns, Bob ! a beauty
    With manners both arch and demure ;
And she 's tall, and her eyes, if you saw them,
    Would remind you of Venice, I 'm sure.

In the nook, just back of the wheel-house,
    We talked of things joyous and grave,
Saw the waters grow dark in the twilight,
    And the moon's silver bridge cross the wave.
The rest is the usual story,
    Which no one knows better than you.

We 'll be married to-night, and I 'll pause here,
   And write you some more when we 're through.

Postscript.

Well ! it 's done, Bob ! and would you believe it ?
   She knows all about that affair,—
And that *was* the Browns' party,—great Cæsar !
   They did us up *Brown,* I declare !
And I love her the more (but this follows,
   Of course, when such cases arise),
For I 've married—just think !—*my own widow.*
   Je—rusalem ! ! Yours, Jack Vansize.

MADELINE ON BASE-BALL.

WHAT a number of nicely dressed people ! I 'm
    awfully glad that we came,
And you 'll be surprised when you find that I 'm
    posted so well on the game.
Those buff-colored shirts and red stockings are
    lovely, I know that they 'll win ;
And that little man there must be short-stop, for his
    head would n't come to my chin.

Those three cushions down in the meadow, I sup-
    pose, are to sit on and rest,
If they had them up here 't would be nicer ; just
    see how that woman is dressed !
The one with the crimson plush mantle, and the
    hat with the ribbons and plume ;
I 've been watching that couple this long time, I 'm
    sure they 're a bride and a groom.

Now, why does the pitcher feel of the ball, every
    time he commences to throw ?
To see if its properly curved ? And the catcher,
    poor man ! he 's consumptive, I know,

Or why does he wear that great pad on his chest?
    Did you hear those men laugh? I declare!
It makes me quite nervous and frightened, and
    look at them now! how they stare!

There 's Alice and George just arriving; that 's her
    trick, always coming in late,
Oh, Vanitas Van-Vanitorum! please see if my hat
    is on straight!
What 's that? Struck a fowl? Oh! how could he?
    That man has no feeling or sense,
Poor little thing! I don't see it, it must have crept
    under the fence.

Stole what? Stole a base? Well! I wonder such
    things are allowed on the ground!
And where on earth has he put it? And what will
    he do when it 's found?
Caught napping at second? Poor fellow! he must
    have been frightfully tired.
There 're the Smiths over there in a landau—is it
    theirs, or one that they 've hired?

The red-stockings whitewashed? What nonsense!
    That 's the silliest thing in base-ball:
And why is n't kalsomine better, if they 've got to
    do it at all?
Well! you don't look as if you 'd enjoyed it. I 'll
    wager you 're glad that it 's done,
But 't was awfully nice and exciting—and who, did
    you tell me, had won?

SITTING ON THE STAIR.

"ART going to the ball this eve?"
This was Jack's question, and I grieve
To say, the evening found me there.
On coming down, I picked my way
Between the couples, still or gay,
Who sat upon the stair.

Half down I paused, the days of yore,
The old, old times came back once more.
In the gay turmoil and the glare
I stood and lost myself, and dreamed
I saw *her* face ; once more we seemed
To sit upon the stair

Once more the old sweet things I said ;
In measure swayed her lovely head
To some gay waltz's witching air ;
Though draughts came whistling from above,
I felt no draughts but draughts of love
When sitting on the stair.

The music ceased, I 'll ne'er forget
Its dreamy sadness, lingering yet
   In her dark, moistened eyes, " I swear !
I 'd give the world to-night to see
That girl, who never more by me
   Will sit upon the stair.

Since then I 've climbed the stairs of life,
I 've had my part of toil and strife,
   And "—my sad revery ended there.
For,—first a giggle, then a cough,
Then rose a voice which said, " Come off !
   Don't stand upon the stair ! "

THE BOSTON GIRL.

I TOLD her of a maid whose mind
    Was filled with tender thoughts and fancies,
A lovely being of the kind
    They write about in old romances.
" Knowest thou," said I, " this maiden fair,
    Whose beauty doth my thoughts beguile ? "
She answered with a dreamy air :
        " Well, I should smile ! "

" Her cheeks possess the rose's hue,
    No form is daintier or completer,
No hair so brown, no eyes so blue,
    No mouth is tenderer or sweeter.
The favored youth who gains the hand
    Of this fair girl will ne'er regret it."
With modest grace she added : " And
        Don't you forget it ! "

" O thou dear mistress of my heart !
    My angel ! let me kneel before thee

And say how heavenly sweet thou art,
　And how devoutly I adore thee."
She turned away her lovely head,
　And with a languid look that fired
My soul, in murmured accents said :
　　"You make me tired!"

THE DEATH-BED OF MRS. O'FLAHERTY.

"HEAR me last wurruds ! Faix ! there 's
O'Shaughnessy,
That wurruld's thafe !—owes me ninepince hap-
peny ;
And there 's Phil Coyne, with his decaiving thricks,
Owes me five shillin's ; and there 's Pathrick Free
By that same token owes me two and six,
The craythur ! May the divil howld him fast ! "
" *The ould woman is sinsible to the last !* "

"Give me a dhrop ! Arrah ! where was I thin ?—
And I owe Micky O'Nail wan pound tin,
And Phelim M'Carthy two pounds, and I owe
Three pounds to Jimmy Hone, and Mrs. Flynn
Wan pound sivin shillin's two pince happeny,—no !
'T is two pince and three farthin's, by your laves."
" *Howly St. Pathrick ! Hear now how she raves !* "

THE BEAUTIFUL TIGHT-ROPE DANCER.

I WOULD like to say, beforehand,
   That it always makes me smile,
To watch those travelling agents,
   Who sling the greatest style.
They dress like princes of the blood,
   Yet any man of sense
Can tell a regular gentleman
   From those commercial gents.

I recollect a man named Briggs,
   A certain travelling swell,
When I tended bar at Smithville
   In the Buckingham hotel.
'T was the time when we were boarding
   The star variety show,
With the beautiful tight-rope dancer,
   Signora Delarito.

Now Briggs had been there fifteen days,
  And in the show each night,
Had watched that tight-rope dancer,
  With rapturous delight ;
For on the fair Signora
  He was completely gone,
And for bouquets to sling at her
  His samples lay in pawn.

One night Briggs rigged himself up fine,
  And when the show was o'er,
Went up the stairs, and hung around
  The fair Signora's door.
And when that tight-rope dancer came,
  And waltzed up to her room,
Although what then and there transpired
  Is wrapped in deepest gloom—

We heard an awful crash, and Briggs
  Came flying down the stairs,
Followed closely by a hamper,
  And a trunk and several chairs.
When he reached the bottom landing,
  He was tired and took a rest ;
Then he picked himself up sadly,
  And took the first train West.

Soon a fresh commercial tourist
   Took the road in Briggs' stead ;
And that star variety phalanx
   Skipped their bill, one night, and fled,
And busted up at.Yankton,
   Which I think was their best plan,
And that "beautiful tight-rope dancer,"
   She turned out to be a man.

HOW THEY PAID THE CHURCH DEBT
AT SMITHVILLE.

A T Smithville once, to help the church,
   We gave an amateur play,
And set up " Julius Cæsar "
   In a most astounding way.
The stars were Oscar Johnson,
   Sam Brown, Bill Jones, and me ;
And the way that Jones played Cæsar
   Was a frightful thing to see.

At first the applause was great ; we played
   For all the parts were worth ;
And the audience was n't critical
   And did n't want the earth ;
Till William Jones, as usual,
   Spoiled the play by getting tight,
And the whole thing somehow ended
   In a regular Smithville fight.

We gave them ancient Romans points—
   Except, it must be said,

When Cassius did n't know his part,
   And sang a song instead.
When Brutus' false calves slewed around,
   At which some people talked ;
And the curtain stuck when Cæsar died,
   And the corpse arose and walked.

But when Mark Antony got up
   Where Cæsar's body lay,
To speak the funeral speech, which is
   The best thing in the play,
The audience laughed and roared, and he
   Soon knew the reason why
When he saw the corpse, which sat upright
   And winked with its left eye.

Jones was a most ambitious man,
   And he thought 't was his best chance,
And rising from his bier began
   An original Fejee dance.
Such conduct in a corpse you 'll own
   It was exceeding queer ;
Then Antony, whose speech was spoiled,
   Got straightway on his ear,

And from the rostrum stepped, and went
   To put a head on Bill,
And they two waltzed around the stage
   In a wild and reckless mill.
Then the Roman soldiers somehow,
   In the scrimmage took a hand,

And the Roman populace followed
  With the members of the band.

The audience cheered the Romans on,
  For they thought 't was in the play,
But the truth dawned on their minds about
  The time the stage gave way.
Then some one raised the cry of " fire "
  And turned out all the lights,
And that there row was worse than them
  Old Gladiators' fights.

The language that was used that night
  Would be awful to relate,
And the Romans from that play went home
  In a terribly used-up state.
Seven ears and noses were sewed on,
  And a dozen fractures set,
But we took three hundred dollars in,
  And paid that old church debt.

THE BALLADE OF CAMPANINI DE LANCY.

'TWAS at Smithville, when "Norma" was given
    By De Lancy's Opera Co.;
The assemblage was brilliant and cultured—
    Fifty cents was the price of the show;
And I think that 't was well for Bellini
    That he died several years ago.

What a storm of applause, and what glitter
    Of bright eyes and calcium lights!
When De Lancy, the tenor robusto,
    Came down from the empyrean heights,
Where he soared in his duet with Norma,
    In a cocked hat, a sword, and red tights.

How gayly he winks toward the boxes,
    Where the bank clerk's daughters recline;
Where the plumber sits in his velvet coat,
    And the solitaire pin doth shine
Of the man who owneth a twentieth part
    Of a share in a telephone line.

But why does he start and grow livid,
   As he turns to the orchestra chairs ?
And why does he falter, then dart through the flies,
   And escape down the private back stairs ?
And who is that man whose fish-like eye
   From the front row steadily glares ?

The curtain came down, and the gas-lights
   Went out, and the music was still ;
For that man with the horrible grin,
   Whose gaze made De Lancy ill,
Was the landlord from down in Ohio,
   Where they skipped without paying the bill.

AN ANGEL.

"IS it you, Jack? I thought you 'd unearth me,
For dancing, you know, I don't care,
So I quietly stole from the music,
The laughter and splendor and glare,
For a rest on the cool, dark piazza.
My cigar 's out; come, give me a light!
And I 'll tell you the dream which absorbed me
Out here in the calm summer night.

"The silver-edged mountains of cloudland
Had softened the light of the moon,
And the fire-flies seemed dancing the lanciers
To the ball-room's far-away tune;
The breezes were rustling and whispering
Up there, in the trees overhead,
And there came a faint scent of syringas,
Like the perfume of days that are fled.

"And my thoughts went back to a village
　Somewhere in the hills, to the time
When my hopes and my visions were golden,
　And life had a halo sublime ;
To an old house under the elm trees,
　Which was made, by the romance and mirth
Of a pretty and fanciful maiden,
　The dearest spot on the earth.

"In my dream, Jack ! I saw her, her eyes had
　That same sweet look as of yore,
And I felt for a time all the vanished
　Enchantment surround me once more.
But alas ! the glamour, the magic
　Of youth are faded and lost,
And she—well ! I found she was mortal,
　Though many a heartache it cost.

"And so, I was sitting here dreaming,
　And striving to think that 't was best
That the romance, the freshness were ended,
　That life seemed a pitiful jest.
And how did you like your fair partner ?
　You were sitting alone on the stair,
And that rose which you have there, resembles
　The one that she wore in her hair—

"Yes ! I know she 's vivacious and lovely,
　And that she 's an angel, I own,
But a snare seemed to lurk in her dimples,
　And her laugh had a traitorous tone.

Introduce me ?—well, no ! for the truth is,
    That beautiful vision of light,
That angel of clay, I once worshipped,—
    Is the girl that you danced with to-night."

A SONG OF SIXPENCE.

OH ! sing that song, from out the olden time !
   Whose burden was the "sixpence of the
     crown,"
Glad sign of wealth, those days of deeds sublime,
  And that great king, whose fame is handed
    down,
From age to age, by pockets full of rye,
And that immortal dish, the singing blackbird pie.

The sun was high above the eastern hill,
  Yet, in the royal palace, every room
Was closely curtained, sombre, dark, and still,
  And in the gilded parlor's stately gloom,
By the dim light, which stole through painted
     panes,
Counted the sordid king, his vast, ill-gotten gains.

The tap'stried warriors trembled overhead
  Like threatening ghosts of foes in battle slain,
Unmoved, he counted on, and counting, said :
  "Great Scott ! there is a sixpence short again."

The curtains parted, through the room, unseen,
Stole, like a lovely ghost, his fair, unrivalled queen.

With many a fearful backward glance, she passed
   The banquet hall, which the preceding night
Had filled with stains of wassail, and at last,
   Entered the pantry, like a ray of light,
And there did break her weary fast, with bread
Whiter than   driven snow, with honey thickly
     spread.

Fit subject for a painter, there she stood,
   Her beauty heightened by the quaint array
Of barrels, drawers, and tins of all things good,—
   But hush ! a step was heard to come that way ;
She shrank with fear, her very heart was stilled,
Pale grew that dimpled cheek, with bread and
     honey filled.

"Ah, me ! that sixpence of the king !" she cried ;
   "Why did I prospect in the old man's vest ?"
She heard the door slammed to and locked out-
     side ;
   Months passed away, her fate is only guessed ;
Perhaps they found her after many a day,
A skeleton, white bleached, alas ! we cannot say.

Around the palace, so the books agree,
   The royal garden lay, and there, the maid,
As fair a maid as one would wish to see,
   In blue silk gown and hose of ebon shade,

For pastime, hung upon a golden line,
Her festive sovereign's shirts, four ply and super-
    fine.

When, lo ! there came a bird, a bird of prey
    It must have been, though writ "a little bird,"
And bit that sweet maid, that she swooned away ;
    And though what then transpired was never
    heard,
O ! thrice unhappy maid ! we know, too well,
That the sweet scent of flowers thou nevermore
    didst smell.

And they are gone, aye ! ages long ago,
    King, queen, and maid, their very graves un-
    known ;
The royal palace, like last April's snow,
    Has vanished, nor is left a single stone ;
And all their wealth and beauty, power and fame,
Are but a mournful tale, an empty, idle name.

JONATHAN BLAKE'S CLOCK.

CARVED with impossible figures, a massive and
    curious timepiece
Stood, in colonial years, by Jonathan Blake's ample
    fireplace—
Stood there, ghostly and grim, with a flintlock and
    sword crossed above it,
And, till the date of this story, at sundown the
    fourteenth of August,
Seventeen seventy-and-seven, the time of the siege
    of Fort Stanwix,
Ancient, stately, and quaint, from its case like an
    old Gothic castle,
Ticked away, without ceasing, in solemn, harmoni-
    ous cadence.

Jonathan Blake's pretty daughter Dorothy sat by
    the window,
Turning a flax-wheel and singing, but paused, as
    with terrible clatter
Open the door flew and in rushed a score of red-
    coated soldiers,

And from the cellar to rafters, seeking a fugitive
    prisoner,
Turned over tables and chairs and fathomed dark
    corners with bayonets.
Rosy the flush that succeeded the pallor of Dorothy's
    cheek, when,
Finding him not, they relinquished their search and
    departed.
Then, with supreme indignation, hiding her maid-
    enly fears, and
Drawing herself up as high as a rather small figure
    permitted,
She, to the humble excuses preferred by the English
    lieutenant,
Answered with all the disdain that a pair of dark
    eyes could exhibit.
Now comes the wonderful part of the tale, for be-
    fore they had vanished
Over the hill by the river, the door of the clock flew
    wide open ;
Forth from its cavernous chamber, in uniform tat-
    tered and blood-stained,—
Forth, like a shadow, a youth stole, and knelt at
    the feet of the maiden,
Kissing her hand, and then like a shadow swiftly
    departed.

Jonathan Blake was rich. His waving cornfields,
    his woodlands
Stretched by the beautiful Mohawk and faded away
    in the distance.

Jonathan Blake was rich, and Jonathan sorely was
 troubled—

Troubled beholding the havoc wrought by those
 red-coat marauders,—

Wrought overnight, and discovered at dawn of the
 following morning.

Grain bins were emptied, the cornfields were tram-
 pled as though by an army,

Haystacks lay smoking in ashes, and oxen and
 horses had vanished.

Sadly he reckoned his loss, and hoping for some
 compensation,

Rashly determined to start for St. Leger's camp at
 Fort Stanwix,

Twenty-one miles up the river, and fifteen miles
 through the forest.

Little lame Solomon Pitkin, a scheming and envious
 neighbor,

Afterwards found to have been for months in the
 pay of the British,

Volunteered to go with him, and so they departed
 together.

Never returned from that journey, Jonathan Blake
 or his comrade.

Whether waylaid by the red-men, or carried off by
 the English,

Tidings there came not ; and never, though long
 and patiently sought, was

Found the magnified treasure with which report had
 possessed him,—

Hundreds and hundreds of dollars, 't was rumored,
  in gold and in silver.

Floating southward, the white clouds, like souls of
  the days of the summer,
Sank o'er the blue hills, the heavens grew cheerless
  and wintry, the bleak winds
Moaned through the lonely gorges and leafless
  boughs of the forest.
So came the winter and passed, and the pretty and
  fanciful maiden
Changed to the staid Mistress Hawthorne, the wife
  of the fugitive prisoner,
Roger Hawthorne, the youth whom the treacherous
  maiden delivered,
Only to render tenfold a captive unto her bright
  eyes.
Though as a timepiece its worth had departed since
  Jonathan's journey,
Still the old clock in its corner, with queer and
  fidgety manner,
Ticked as if it possessed some deep and mysterious
  secret ;
And as the years passed away, in the darkness of
  evening its quaint voice
Often brought back to the lovers the time when
  the slender young ensign,
Wedged in its coffin-like chamber, his ruthless pur-
  suers evaded.

Years rolled on, and the Hawthornes—their children and children's children—

Peacefully slept in the church-yard, unknown in the
    beautiful city,

Reared on the spot where their dwelling stood in
    the whispering forest.

Long since, the loving tradition about the old clock
    had departed.

Owned by some careless descendant, it slumbered
    away in the attic,

Covered with lumber and dust ; until, asking for
    just such a timepiece,

Came to his door, at dusk one day, a mysterious
    stranger,

Bent, and lame in one leg, a little old man in knee-
    breeches,

With a cunning and sinister eye, and dusty, black,
    thread-bare apparel,

Who, when the price of the dingy and ponderous
    relic was settled,

Paid it in queer old silver, and shut himself up in
    the attic.

After the noise of a hammer and chisel some time
    had resounded,

Suddenly all was still, and they who ascended to
    seek him

Found the clock lying in fragments, but where
    was the singular stranger?

Lo ! the old man had departed in some unaccount-
    able manner.

Strewn with pieces of paper, from end to end, was
    the attic,—

Remnants of hundreds of bank-notes, thin and
    yellow and faded ;

Currency Continental, worthless for all but old
    paper ;
Torn as by one disappointed, and scattered about
    in madness.

All that remains to be told of this far-stretched,
    curious story,
Is that, repaired and revarnished, the stately and
    veteran timepiece,
That since old Jonathan's journey had been in a
    state of disorder,
Ticked away, as of yore, with solemn, harmonious
    cadence.

"THE LUCK OF GEORGE McCLURE."

I.

'TWAS a year ago, coming December,
  You remember the evening, I know.
We were sitting right here, by the hearth fire,
  And watching its flicker and glow,
You and I, George McClure and Jack Lyndon,
  Right here, in the Calumet Club,
The sanctum and innermost temple
  Of Beacon Hill and the "Hub."

II.

And George owned the tender impeachment,
  And told in his spiciest way,
His conquest of little Sue Slater,
  The prettiest girl of the day.
What a color Sue had! and her figure!
  So rich, yet petite, and what eyes!
How lucky he was! how we envied
  The scapegrace his beautiful prize!

III.

Sue was poor, but she sang at St. Agnes'
   For twenty-five hundred a year,
Three-fourths of which went to a parent
   Who never was seen about here.
A cultured and delicate person,
   Who travelled around for her health ;
I saw her last summer at Newport,
   Attired like a lady of wealth.

IV.

She told me that she was Sue's mamma,
   And spoke of her dear daughter Sue,
Which, as that was the name of Sue's mother,
   Was, strictly and honestly, true.
She was forty years old, so she told us
   With childish, ingenuous air,
But she might, in so far as her looks went,
   Have been her own mother, I swear !

V.

Well ! George had just squandered his fortune,
   And used up his sister's besides,
When his cousin John got him that clerkship,
   A something or other in hides.
But George was n't fashioned for labor ;
   It all ended up in a row,
And he left, and some say he was kicked out,
   But that does n't matter just now.

VI.

It was just after that, that George met me,
  And said there was "really no choice
But to marry that little Sue Slater,
  And manage to live on her voice."
But his Beacon Street friends would n't have it,
  And chipped in, and sent him out West,
To Los Angeles, near the Pacific,
  For a long recreation and rest.

VII.

He wrote me last month, and he mentioned
  The fruits and the wonderful air,
And how he had met a rich widow,
  And hoped that poor Sue would n't care.
Last Friday I heard from him further,
  By telegram (ninety cents due).
"When you see this," it read, "we 'll be married;
  Please break it to poor little Sue."

VIII.

To bear such a message was cruel,
  A task not at all to my mind,
But I saw her, and managed the business
  In a way that was gentle and kind.
While I told her she seemed to be laughing.
  These women are strange, I declare !
And it struck me somehow, from her manner,
  That she knew all about the affair.

IX.

There was surely some secret ; she giggled,
    And blushed, and at last out it came,—
George, it seemed, had been fooled by cosmetics,
    Misled by the difference in name,
And at last, in his search for an heiress,
    That one ruling thought of McClure's,
He had married Sue's Grandmother. Waiter !
    A sour mash and seltzer ! what 's yours ?

THE END.